Anonymous

Stretton of Ringwood Chace

A Novel. Vol. 2

Anonymous

Stretton of Ringwood Chace
A Novel. Vol. 2

ISBN/EAN: 9783337273590

Printed in Europe, USA, Canada, Australia, Japan

Cover: Foto ©Andreas Hilbeck / pixelio.de

More available books at **www.hansebooks.com**

STRETTON OF RINGWOOD CHACE.

A NOVEL.

"There is a Power above which shapes our ends,
Rough-hew them as we may."—SHAKSPEARE.

IN THREE VOLUMES.

VOL. II.

[LONDON:]
HURST AND BLACKETT, PUBLISHERS,
SUCCESSORS TO HENRY COLBURN,
13, GREAT MARLBOROUGH STREET.

1860.

STRETTON OF RINGWOOD CHACE.

CHAPTER I.

THE extreme heat continued, often render-
ing it impossible for the girls to meet at
all, short as was the distance between their
homes. One very sultry day, when they were
thus kept apart, and Arthur, absorbed in
some difficult drawing, was less sociable than
usual, Mabel had spent the morning alone,
lounging luxuriously with a book under the
great trees, which came up close to the east
end of the house. At length, having finished

her book, she went in at the window, for the purpose of changing it.

The library, and Mrs. Stretton's business-room, with the matted passage dividing them, formed the east end of the Chace-house; the library running along the south front, Mrs. Stretton's room looking north. The entrance to this last was at the end of the passage furthest from the hall; the library, which was longer than the passage, opened from the central hall itself.

It was the loftiest and best-proportioned room in the house. It was lined with book-shelves, which accommodated themselves to its various odd recesses. The three side windows were so deeply sunk in the wall, and so shadowed by the intertwined creepers as to be ornamental rather than useful. But the semi-circular end, farthest from the door, formed one great cluster window, of five divisions, looking sideways to the flower-garden, and opening with two shallow stone steps to the turf slope, shadowed by great trees, which here came up to the house, and fell gradually to the park.

While Mabel was standing at the book-shelves near the door, which happened to be ajar, she suddenly heard the voice of her Italian maid, raised high in dispute. (Bianca, through the pertinacious teaching of her young mistress, was at last beginning to speak in-telligible English.)

"The Signorina! it belongs to the Signo-rina! No one shall take my young lady's letters to her but me!"

A letter was still a great event to Mabel, who, indeed, had no one to write to her but Clara. She went eagerly out into the hall.

Old Thomas was coming down the matted passage from Mrs. Stretton's room. On an old-fashioned silver salver he bore a letter, which Mrs. Stretton, to whom he had just taken the post-bag, had given him to deliver to Miss Arleigh. This he was defending

B 2

with mastiff-like fidelity from Bianca, whose large black eyes were flashing with excitement.

" I will always take all the Signorina's letters to her my own self! Some day shall she have love-letters ; then I take, I bring ! *You* touch them ?—You so much as look at them ?—No !"

The sonorous voice in which she proclaimed her intentions, for the benefit of the whole house, and within ear-shot of Mrs. Stretton's private room, certainly did not promise Mabel very effectual aid in carrying out any future clandestine correspondence.

As soon as the young lady appeared, old Thomas quietly relinquished the letter to Bianca, who approached her mistress in triumph. But ere she had well delivered it, she exclaimed, in tones between despair and entreaty—

" Ah, Signorina ! her hair !—She will favour me, when she shall have read her letter, she will come to her chamber, where I may dress it anew."

" Nonsense, Bianca! don't tease me about my hair now !" said Mabel, impatiently. She passed back through the library, and out upon the shady turf, the letter in her hand.

This same hair of Mabel's was at once the pride and the despair of the Italian maid. It was so bright, so abundant, so really beautiful, taking a different tint every way she brushed it ; and yet so *English*, so intractable, so any-thing but silky or amenable ; not having suffi-cient natural curl to keep it in order without further trouble ; but just enough to give to every lock, almost every hair, its own especial bend and wave, independent of the rest, and wholly irrespective of the demands of fashion, or even the laws of uniformity.

" All very well for saints and angels in an altar-piece," murmured Bianca; " only she resembles them not in the face. The saints she resembles in no point; those look always

so sad and quiet,—even the angels very little.
Angels smile often, but laugh never ; and one
sees in her look that she would laugh any
minute, though she had been crying the
minute before. And yet she always looks
like some picture; now one, now another,—
which, I cannot tell."

Mabel, meanwhile, had opened her letter.

The direction was so hurried and irregular,
so different from Clara's bold, decided hand,
that, till she had broken the seal, she could
scarcely believe it to be hers. It was only a
few lines, and ran as follows :

" DEAREST MAB,

" I am going to be married. I did not
like that any one should tell you of it but
myself. It is to Dr. Harland ; you saw him,
if you remember, the winter before last, when
poor little Fred had that terrible fever. Wish
me joy, though I don't expect to *have* it.
Not that it will be *his* fault if I do not; but

it is a strange, uncomfortable affair altogether, and I cannot tell what to make of it.

"Ever yours affectionately,

"CLARA STRETTON.

"P.S.—I shall have two little stepdaughters, but I cannot fancy that I shall ever like them, so you need not be jealous. I never did properly like any child except you."

"Not like children!" was Mabel's first exclamation. This last sentence seemed more bewildering to her than all the rest. "Why, at school she could hardly learn her lessons for the little ones hanging about her. And then at home, with the boys! Oh, what will they all do without her?"

"And then"—as she referred again to the letter—"why doesn't she like it? It cannot be the children really;—but he is much older than she is, I suppose. But why does she marry him then?"

And Mabel, walking, in her excitement,

rapidly hither and thither among the trees, tried to remember all she could about Dr. Harland. She particularly wished to recollect what he was like; but no distinct image could she summon up. Poor Fred had been very dangerously ill; and she, like all the rest, had been very much frightened; and when the "doctor"—sent for express from town, at the desire of the usual medical attendant—at length arrived, every one in the house had felt a heavy weight removed : a painful sense of personal responsibility lifted off. But even the "doctor" was no magician ; the boy certainly did not die, which had become every-one's daily dread ; but not till after a week or more had elapsed, was he undeniably a shade better. At last, Dr. Harland had pronounced him out of danger. During this weary period of suspense, all personal interest in the doctor had been merged in anxiety for the patient. Mabel, too, had been strictly excluded from the sick-room. She had indeed crept into it on tiptoe, during Dr. Harland's first visit, to hear what he would say about Fred; but had been summarily ejected by Edward, who carried her out bodily, locked her in a distant room, and then hurried back to hear the physician's verdict; returning, however, very quickly, to tell her that they hoped Fred would not die; and to set her free, on promise of future obedience to quarantine regulations.

She now, indeed, recollected that after Dr. Harland's last visit to Fred, who was then fast recovering, nurse had sent her to ask Miss Clara for something she was in want of; —that supposing the doctor to be with her in the drawing-room, she had at first entered timidly; but finding no one there, had passed quickly through to the library—a smaller and snugger room, between the drawing-room and the well-warmed conservatory—where Clara often spent her winter mornings. Mabel now distinctly recalled the aspect of the room that

bitter cold day : the table drawn close to the
fire; Clara's little writing-desk, which she had
pushed across to Dr. Harland, who had followed her into the room to write a prescrip-
tion, and who now sat, quite in shadow, with
his back to the window, holding to the fire
the freshly-written paper ; Clara sitting on the
other side of the fire, into which she was
fixedly gazing.

It was a dark winter afternoon ; yet Mabel
remembered seeing by the firelight Clara's
open account-book on the table ; the books—
a novel and some travels—which she had
been reading, heaped up beside her; and a
large half-opened brown-paper parcel, of boys'
books, from which she had been selecting
something to amuse Fred. The light had
shone, too, on Clara's face as she looked up,
glanced on her polished black hair, and flick-
ered into her deep black eyes, which looked
darker and far heavier than usual, from
anxious watchings by her little brother. To

the same cause Mabel had at the time attributed something peculiar in her whole look. But Dr. Harland's face, which she now strained her memory to conjure up, she had positively not seen at all. Clara had risen at once, made a hasty apology, and left the room with Mabel, who, with her usual shyness, had been only too glad to make her escape, without once looking round. " Provoking !" she now thought, " not even to know what Clara's husband is like !" And then she returned to her old thought : " What will they do without her ?"

For some time she paced restlessly up and down in the shade, absorbed in these somewhat self-tormenting reveries. Then she roused herself, and saying, half aloud, " I had better go and tell my aunt," she once more passed through the library, and went slowly down the matted passage to Mrs. Stretton's room.

Her knock was answered by a " come

in !" — and she entered, like one in a dream.

The room had looked dull on that dreary autumn evening when Mabel had first beheld it; it looked sombre even now, this glowing Midsummer noontide. It was low and wainscoted, and insufficiently lighted by its two casemented windows, small-paned and heavy-mullioned, which looked out on the gravel of the from platform, and northwards, through a gap in the dark foliage, to Ringwood village and church.

Mrs. Stretton was sitting at her papers, much as she had sat the evening of Mabel's arrival. Mabel now stood still before her, and began at once :—

" Aunt !—Clara is going to be married."

She held Clara's letter in her hand, but did not offer it. A sight of the occasional letters she had received had never been offered, or asked for.

" Whom is it to, my dear ?" asked Mrs.

Stretton. Her tone indicated that she made the inquiry simply from a certain sense of courtesy to Mabel—not from the slightest interest in the question.

" To a Dr. Harland," replied Mabel. " They said, when he was sent for to Fred, that he was very famous."

" Certainly, my dear; a very eminent physician; I know him well by repute," said Mrs. Stretton, with more animation. " A very excellent match, my dear Mabel. Dr. Harland visits in the first circles; and Miss —Mrs. Harland—will be introduced into society quite above what she could ever have aspired to otherwise."

" My poor Clara !" said Mabel—" I wish I could see her !"

" I think it is very possible you *may* see her now, my love. How old are you, Mabel ?"

" Fifteen next birthday, aunt."

She was very little more than fourteen, but

was still child enough to make the most of her age.

" Very well. When you are eighteen, you know you will be in London, to be presented."

" *I* presented ?" said Mabel, looking bewildered.

" Of course, my dear. All young ladies of your station must be presented. They would otherwise be unable to take that position to which they are entitled."

Mabel gave a nod of assent.

" Very well, aunt ; that is all right. Only, I may come back here directly, may I not ?"

" What do you mean ?" said Mrs. Stretton, looking puzzled. " Of course we shall spend the season in London, for you to be properly introduced."

" I shall not like that at all," said Mabel, decidedly.

" What do you mean ?" again asked her aunt.

" Why," said Mabel, "everybody here knows the Chace ; and when they see me they know that I belong to it. But the daughters of the great people who go up to London won't want me for a companion, and nobody will know or care anything about the Chace, or me either."

Mrs. Stretton looked rather struck.

" I very much agree with you, Mabel," she said, after a short silence. " You have the right spirit in you, child."

" And Clara ?" asked Mabel.

" Why, you know, my dear, we must be in London a little while for the presentation ; and I will take care that you have opportunities of seeing your friend. Marrying as she does, I shall no longer hesitate, especially as the name—" she checked herself.

" But that is so long to wait," said Mabel.

" My dear ! I *cannot* let *you* go and *stay* with any one. I should be most happy if your friends would visit *me*. Shall I ask them again ?"

" They will not come," said Mabel.

" Then, my dear, be happy ; you *are* happy here, are you not, Mabel?"

" Oh yes, aunt ! And I love Ringwood so much ! It is the nicest place, I think, in the world !"

" Then go now, dear, and write to your friend all you want to say. You are a good, true-hearted little thing !"

And she kissed her with such unwonted affection as brought the tears into Mabel's eyes, and sent her, in a mood unusually soft-ened, to write her congratulations and en-quiries to Clara.

CHAPTER II.

CLARA, meanwhile, seemed to be doing her best to render Mabel's often-repeated question —" What will they do without her?" as easy as possible of solution. If it had been possible to attribute to *her* any notions of predetermined self-abnegation, or voluntary martyrdom, she might have been deemed heroically bent upon reconciling her father and brothers to her loss, by making herself as little to be regretted as possible. In fact, ever since her engagement had been a settled thing, she had

been thoroughly *cross*. The boys plainly
stated their opinion, that it would be a good
thing when sister Clara was married and off;
there was no doing anything to please her.
They looked on her, however, with unwonted
awe, as having in some way passed out of their
sphere. Her most unreasonable reprimands
were received with unprecedented submission;
and a sort of deference pervaded their whole
manner towards her. To Dr. Harland their
feeling was one of unmitigated hostility, only
suppressed by fear.

" It's all your fault, Fred," said John, with
much asperity; " if you hadn't been ill, we
should never have had him here; and we should
have gone on comfortably, as we did before."

" I'm sure," was Fred's ungrateful reply,
" I didn't want them to have him for me. I
should have got well a great deal sooner without any of that horrid stuff. And ordering
me to keep still, and not talk! and starving
me besides!" added Fred, quite viciously,

working himself into a passion with the recollection of his wrongs.

Mr. Stretton even said to Clara, with some
impatience :—

" My dear, if the thought of this marriage
makes you so uncomfortable, you had better
let me break it off. I will settle everything;
you know I do not want to part with you. A
great deal too much difference in age; I
thought so from the first."

·" Why, papa," exclaimed Clara,—" what
do you call difference in age? You know I
am two-and-twenty. It is not as if I were a
young girl."

" Oh no, certainly !" said Mr. Stretton,
his gravity relaxing in spite of himself.—
" And he is"—

" Oh, quite as young for a man as two-and-
twenty for a woman."

" I don't quite know that," said Mr.
Stretton, quietly. " However, my dear, you
must do it on your own responsibility. I have

no objection, as I told you, further than that; only let me see you happy."

"Oh, I suppose I shall be as happy as other people; one does not expect to be so very happy in this world!"—And with this edifying remark, and a half-apologetic kiss, she left the room.

"I really cannot think what is the matter with your sister," remarked Mr. Stretton to his son, as they sat together after dinner. "I asked her this morning if she began to think the difference in age too great, and she wouldn't hear of it. Yet it *is* too much; I have disliked it all along. And Dr. Harland is not even young-looking of his age, though he is such a handsome man. And *that* would be no recommendation to Clara," Mr. Stretton remarked, as if thinking aloud. "She always disliked handsome men particularly."

"I have no patience with her," exclaimed Edward; "it is all her ridiculous pride. And she is making herself and everybody else uncomfortable. And too bad to Harland too! I will tell her my mind about it." And Edward rose from table.

"My dear boy, do not annoy your sister," remonstrated Mr. Stretton.

"I really cannot have things go on so any longer!" said Edward; "it is unbearable!" And he went into the drawing-room; where he found Clara trying over one piece of music after another, making discord instead of harmony by her impatient attempts.

"It is really absurd to bring me such difficult music! Enough to set one against the thing altogether!"

Clara, though she played well, had no particular taste for music; but Dr. Harland was passionately fond of it; and at *her* request, had brought her some of his favourites to try.

"I am really ashamed of you, Clara!" said her brother, almost passionately. "A sister of mine to accept a man she does not love!

and for the sake of such paltry notions,
too !"

" Not *love ?*"—exclaimed Clara starting up,
her eyes flashing fire. Then suddenly she sat
down again, laughing.

" Oh, *that* is what you are all afraid of, is
it ?—Now, Edward, don't you think I am
old enough to know my own mind ?"

" Never mind your age," began Edward,
almost laughing in his turn. But Clara interrupted him :—" And what do you mean by
paltry notions ?"

" Now, Clara," said her brother, " you
know you always said that you did not wish
to marry any one in business ; that you would
like a professional man so much better. And
here you are, sacrificing yourself, and taking
Harland in, because you are ashamed of what
your father and brother belong to, and what
you yourself owe everything to in the world."

" My dear Edward," said Clara, suddenly
taking his hand, " how could you ever fancy

such a thing of me? I had forgotten that such absurd notions had ever entered my head. I recollect now that I used to talk in that way when I was young and foolish." Edward looked down, to conceal an inclination to smile. "And very provoking it is, for every one who has ever heard me say so will be sure to think as you do. As if I ever meant that I wished to marry a doctor!— What I have always disliked the thought of, above all things! No peace or comfort, nothing but worries and interruptions; no travelling, or enjoying oneself!—Always staying at home, looking at the same carpets and curtains."

"Then why do you do it?" asked Edward, dryly.

"And then to be a stepmother," said Clara, conveniently not hearing his question. "Another thing I have always had a horror of."

"Two tame little girls, *vice* John and Fred, to say nothing of that scapegrace, Mabel.

The little town birds won't be as wild as our country ones."

"No!" said Clara; "he says they have pined, as it were, since their mother died— grown pale and fretful; I am sure they do him no credit. But doctors' children always are sickly, and their wives too—no wonder! And then to live in London, which is like being in prison."

"If you make yourself very agreeable, perhaps we may have you down here sometimes; not if you are as cross as you have been lately."

"What will be the use of being down here, when he is obliged to be in London with his tiresome patients?"

"Really, Miss Clara, you are too complimentary. However, it is clear that you have a hard life before you; so let us have tea, there's a darling, and be comfortable while we can. You know that Dr. Harland cannot be down this evening, so you

may be as happy as if nothing had happened."

From that day, though Clara's crossness, in
a somewhat modified form, still continued,
both father and brother merely laughed at it;
especially as they observed that Dr. Harland
watched with a sort of amused enjoyment any
manifestation which took place in his presence.
To *him* Clara was *not* cross ; only distant and
reserved.

To do Clara justice, however, this same
crossness had been throughout of a very super-
ficial character; but to one of her disposition
there was something indescribably mortifying
in acknowledging herself constrained, as it
were, to do what she had always declared she
would never do; and this not on one point
only, but several; in finding her own involuntary feelings too strong for the firm will,
the steady judgment, on which, with some
justice, she had before prided herself. How
much an irrepressible yearning to be a mother

to the motherless children, had really influenced her acceptance of the father, she, at least, never guessed.

Her first thought, however, had been of those whom she was about to leave; and she had positively declined entering into the engagement at all, until satisfied that her place at home was likely to be in some measure supplied.

Her father, unwilling, perhaps, to dwell upon the thought of parting with her, had at first put her off, saying, "Make your mind easy, my dear, and consider only your own happiness in the matter; we will manage somehow or other." Finding, however, that she persisted in refusing any positive answer to Dr. Harland until satisfied on the subject of home arrangements, he at last said, "Well, I suppose, Edward, we must persuade Aunt Sarah to come and take care of us." This was unanimously pronounced a bright idea, and one which, if it could only be carried into execution, would solve the problem before them more satisfactorily than could have been hoped.

"Aunt Sarah," as she was always called in the family, was Mr. Stretton's only sister, some few years younger than himself. She had been more than commonly beautiful; and even now, despite her silvered hair, "*lovely*" would have been the natural epithet to apply to her. Of course, various stories, all more or less doleful, were afloat, to account for her not having married. There was probably some amount of truth in one or all of these stories; yet nothing could have been less doleful than the individual respecting whom they were circulated. Her equable, unruffled cheerfulness, which even in youth had seldom risen to high spirits, had no doubt much contributed to her long retention of beauty.

At the death of her last surviving parent, Aunt Sarah had been warmly pressed by her brother to make his house her home; his wife, to whom she was strongly attached, joining

earnestly in the request. But she shrank
with something of that pride which was inhe-
rent in the whole family, from entering a
circle already complete in itself, where a place
was offered to her from kind consideration
only; so she retained as her abode the pretty
cottage in which her parents' latter years had
been spent. There, with the perfect content
belonging to her character, she found sufficing
interests for herself in reading and garden-
ing, in needlework of every sort, and in the
favourite accomplishment of her girlhood,
painting wild flowers from nature;—was a good
neighbour, and always ready to do a kindness
in any direction. But she had no marked
intellectual tastes, was too refined for gossip,
and lacked that superabundant energy which
happily enables some to make for themselves a life's work in teaching children,
or visiting the poor. So, now that she was
really wanted — now that a place was va-
cant which she alone could fill—she was

not reluctant to accede to her brother's appeal.

It was a joyful day when her consent was received.

"Then, Edward, you may go to as many balls as you like, and leave us to talk over old times together," said his father; "you can't expect, you know, to get me out much, when I have no longer this girl to look after and keep out of mischief," and he patted Clara's head as he spoke.

"Madam Clara will be having receptions of her own," said Edward; "which you will have to attend, and see her play the matron."

"And chaperon to my two daughters," said Clara, with some of her old fun in her eyes.

The only question seemed to be, how one so gentle as Aunt Sarah could cope, in holiday times, with the boys, accustomed to Clara's somewhat stormy reign. Edward, however, who had been a good deal with his aunt in his childhood, declared that, mild as she was, she had as much *will* as any Stretton of them all (he rather piqued himself on the family characteristic); a will that seemed, indeed, in her case, to have in it something of magic. Whatever Aunt Sarah made up her mind to, was infallibly accomplished; seemingly without effort on her part, or resistance on that of others. She had made *him* mind, he averred, and that was saying enough.

He had been always rather a favourite of hers, for a reason which she once unguardedly alluded to in his presence, little guessing how much their good understanding would thereby be endangered. One day, when Edward, then a schoolboy of eleven, happened to be in the room, his aunt laughingly remarked to her brother that she was glad he had at least one child a true Stretton, with fair hair and complexion; and not a little was she startled, when the boy, colouring scarlet to the roots of his hair, bounced indignantly out of the room, banging the door after him. Mr. Stretton could not be easy till he had followed and pacified his boy; but he afterwards laughed, and explained to his sister that this complexion, which even in a girl would have been remarked as fair, was poor Edward's bugbear, the shame of his life, the last resource (to her shame be it spoken) of that saucy brunette Clara, when worsted in some war of words. Not till the sun and storm of another half-year had passed over his head, was he fully reconciled to his aunt.

In process of time, however, they had become staunch allies. She indeed felt a peculiar pride and interest in her eldest nephew, the future representative of the family; for something of the Stretton nature slumbered beneath her placid mien and quiet deportment. And it was by her that Edward had first been taught to love the quartered Stretton shield and flying arrow—a quaint

representation of which her grandfather had
brought with him, his only earthly inheritance,
to the great metropolis; and bequeathed, with
so much of far more tangible value, to his
descendants.

Clara insisted, and it was at length agreed,
that the wedding should be deferred until
Aunt Sarah could become a member of their
family circle. " I could not manage without
her," was the argument by which she at last
carried her point. So it was settled, after
some consultation and correspondence, that
Aunt Sarah should hasten, as much as possible,
her final removal from the home of so many
years, should give Clara all the help in her
power, and remain permanently to fill her
place. What regrets she felt, what old associations were painfully revived by this breaking
up of her home, could only be guessed. It
was not her way to talk of her own feelings ;
and she knew her brother well enough to be

sure that, the pain of the moment once over, she would never have cause to regret the change. In that assurance she was not disappointed.

CHAPTER III.

THE long talked-of step had been taken; Arthur was now definitely established at a large school, some way off, to take his chance, and learn to take his own part, among other boys. The parting between him and Mabel had been rather a doleful affair. Mrs. Stretton took his departure, as she took everything, with grave quietness. The mortifications and disappointments of her early years, operating upon a character naturally both proud and strong, had, perhaps, greatly contributed to render habitual this self-contained demeanour. Whether they had rendered her callous, may be doubted; but they had certainly deadened in her that buoyancy of hope, and ardour of enjoyment, which make sorrow, by contrast, so much the more keenly felt.

She now only devoted herself with renewed energy to her avocations as Lady of the Manor, from which Arthur alone had occasionally been able to beguile her. And, in truth, the task imposed upon her by her position was no light one. Nearly the whole of Colonel Ashgrove's fortune had been sunk in the purchase of an estate, not at the best very profitable, and at that time thoroughly impoverished by years of stint and neglect. It had required years of good management to render the property once more self-supporting. And Mrs. Stretton could not adapt herself to circumstances, as some might have done; she had her weaknesses — *feminine* weaknesses they would generally be called,—which allowed her scarcely fair play in this battle with adverse fate.

D 2

Neither the estate which her ancestors had held before her, nor the tenants, whose fathers had been *their* tenants, must receive injury at her hands. She *could* not cut down the magnificent timber for sale, nor clear away the thickly-tangled copses, to afford more space for agriculture; she could not abolish the stately herds of deer, to replace them by animals of a more profitable description. Not a stone, not a beam of the old house must moulder from neglect, while that house was *her* home. Nor, unindulgent as was her character, sturdy as was her assertion of what she deemed her own just claims, *could* she distress for rent a tenant whose disabling sickness or unmerited difficulties she had herself witnessed. She could not let the meanest tenement on her estate want needful repairs, so long as it was the abode of a human being.

And now, in the place of her lost son, she had taken upon herself the charge of *two*

children—and one of them *a girl!* Arthur,
of course, would have the estate, and ought,
however poor, to be therewith content; and
for a younger brother some shift might have
been found—India, or the Church! But Mrs.
Stretton knew too well, by personal expe-
rience, the mortifications and privations of a
portionless woman's lot, willingly to expose to
such a fate the niece for whom she had made
herself responsible.

But while Mrs. Stretton's increased absorp-
tion in the management of her affairs arose in
part from anxiety for Mabel's future prospects,
it of course tended to render her niece's life,
for the time being, still more solitary and
monotonous.

Fräulein C., however, had now returned, to
resume the superintendence of Mabel's doings;
and between her and her pupil two new points
of sympathy, or, rather, of companionship, had
fortunately arisen.

When Mabel, on the return of the gover-

ness from her vacation, had immediately com-
municated to her, as the great news of the
day, Clara's approaching marriage, Fräulein
C.'s first remark had been :—

"Then the Fräulein will now, doubtless,
stick—work—something—to a wedding present for her friend?"

Mabel's eyes sparkled.

"But I work so badly!" she said.

"Courage! I will help! And that will
certainly go right well!" replied the good-
natured German.

"Only not knitting!" said Mabel, with a
half-comic shiver.

"My child, no!—You shall embroider
something right pretty; and the friend will
so heartily take pleasure therein!"

And the pocket-handkerchief, begun under
these auspices, bade fair to become a miracle
of success under difficulties.

"Well, mein Fräulein, and what shall the
device be?"

The governess was seated in state, at the head of the heavy school-table; a film of cob-web muslin in her hand ; a book of patterns open before her.

"Oh ! first, let there be a wreath of oak-leaves—with acorns, if you can ; that is what Clara likes best, I know. She always looked so beautiful, like a queen, when she put a wreath of oak-leaves in her hair !"

"Ah ! well, as it pleases you, my child ! That will be difficult in the working; but— we will see. Now, for the corners?"

" Her name must be in one corner."

" Without doubt. But which name?"

"I will only put ' *Clara ;*' she is always ' Clara' to me. Ah ! please, put—' Mabel to Clara.' "

" Good ! that sounds well—touching. But for both names in one corner will room not find itself. Of necessity must we put ' Mabel' in one corner."

Mabel could not quite repress a laugh.

"Eh! what is that, my child? What is amiss?"

"Dear friend, I beg your pardon. Yes, that will do very well, I think—'Mabel' in one"—She could not trust her voice to go on, lest the stifled laughter should break forth.

"Right good; and 'to Clara' in the other. You comprehend me now right well. But there should also not wholly fail some sign—some token—of the friend's new name; of this happy event. The—what do you call them?—the—*Chiffern*—in one corner should these also appear."

"Very well," said Mabel. "'C. H.' Very pretty initials; they will look very nice for the third corner. But what shall we have for the fourth? Oh! now I have it!—The Stretton Arrow! with the motto below it—'Straight on!' It will be very difficult, but I do not mind the trouble. Nothing can suit Clara so well!"

"These friends are cousins, then? That knew I not before?" said the governess.

"Why? What makes you think so? I wish they were!"

"Ah! the Arrow is plainly to be seen, when one lives at the Chace. But—you will pardon me, mein Fräulein—I thought—it seemed to me to have heard—that these friends were —I forget the word—*bourgeois.*"

But Mabel's face was crimson.

"You will forgive me, mein Fräulein! What have I said? And, besides, Mr.—the Doctor—Harland—"

"I don't care anything about him; I don't know anything. I only know that the Stretton Flying Arrow *belongs* to Clara; nothing could suit her so well! '*Straight on!*' The words seem made for her! And she shall *have* them, worked on her pocket-handkerchief! If I can only manage the stitches!" Mabel concluded, rather doubtfully.

But Fräulein C. would hear of no doubts.

A German might demur at heraldic difficulties ; but what Frau or Fräulein ever allowed herself to be daunted where needlework was in question ? And her enthusiasm was contagious, as genuine enthusiasm generally is. Mabel began really to enjoy the undertaking, which had at first appeared so formidable.

Not quite so prosperous, at least at the outset, proved the drawing-lessons—the second enterprise in which the governess found her co-operation unexpectedly sought by her pupil.

Mabel soon tired of laboriously copying crayon heads, under Fräulein C.'s superintendence. Steady mechanical application was not her forte ; and after every moderately successful attempt, she only perceived the more clearly how far removed she was from all hope of ever realizing her own ambitious visions.

For Mabel had had daring projects, confided to none, not even to Arthur or Catherine, of reproducing these images of her ancestors, not singly on detached canvasses, but grouped, in action—engaged in the doings which tradition had linked with their names. But though her zeal for the mere practice of drawing waxed lukewarm, as these dazzling dreams melted into thin air, yet an impulse had been given to her natural taste, which set her to study, with fresh interest, the old family pictures scattered throughout the house, and to acquaint herself intimately with each. Now she began to appreciate, with an instinct which her early life had rendered peculiarly acute, the great beauty and value of many of these portraits, as *pictures*.

In the saloon, the one wonderful Holbein, finished like a miniature, yet reproducing, with the merciless fidelity of a modern daguerreotype, every chance blemish, exaggerated instead of softened; subordinating expression wholly to detail—yet so real, so individual, as to seem in remembrance like a face-to-face interview with a living person. In the hall, a stately Vandyck—the cavalier's cobweb lace falling over his gleaming armour; the fingers so white and taper as almost to belie their firm grasp of the sword. There was even a Sir Joshua Reynolds—a sweet sketch of Mrs. Stretton's own mother, just before she was snatched away in the prime of her matronly grace and dignity. Later portraits there were none. A Stretton of Ringwood must be painted only by the first artist of the day; and for such expensive luxuries, it was long, alas! since the necessary funds had been forthcoming.

One morning, before breakfast, as Mabel was in the dining-room, standing in absorbed contemplation before an especial favourite, she was startled by old Thomas's hobbling step; and turning round, saw him close behind her—a crumpled yellow paper in his hand.

"Would you like the list of the pictures, Miss?" he inquired.

Mabel was old Thomas's especial favourite. To Arthur he was deferential, as to all of the blood of Stretton ; but he had never been able to divest himself of a certain feeling of jealousy towards one who took the place, and even bore the name, of " poor Master Arthur." To Mabel, who interfered with no old claims or fixed associations, his services were devoted with unmixed, almost chivalrous loyalty.

Mabel took the list eagerly.

" The list, Miss, that my father had given him by the old squire, when it was his business to show the gentry through the rooms ; for many and many carriage-fuls would come on a Wednesday—(that was the open day, Miss)—to see the pictures, and the bits of woodwork, and the ceilings, and mantelpieces, and the like. But Missus has put a stop to all that. She never liked it, in her

father's time; and would shut herself up in
her own room (that's where you sleeps now,
Miss), directly she heard the sound of car-
riage-wheels, on one of them days."

Mabel, meanwhile, had been glancing rapidly through the list, written in clear,
crabbed, old-fashioned characters, still perfectly legible, though the ink was faded with
time. It was methodically drawn up, in
double columns, the one giving the name of
the individual represented, the other that of
the artist, with the date appended.

"But, Thomas, in this list one of the portraits is said to be by Sir Godfrey Kneller,
and I am sure there is not one in the house
by him. I know what his pictures are like."

"Ah, Miss! that is a sad story! You had
better not say anything about that picture to
your aunt, Miss; she might not like it."

"Why not?" asked Mabel. "Where is
the picture?"

"Oh, that picture has never been here in

my time, Miss, nor my father's neither ; and the family have never much liked to have it spoken about. And I don't know as it's the sort of story to tell you, Miss, neither."

" But where is the picture ?" persisted Mabel.

" Why, Miss, that's what none of us can't say. The old squire, he didn't care much for such things, like ; and Missus never opens her lips about them. We only knows what we hear tell, bit by bit, from the old housekeeper that was here in my father's time, Miss.—But there comes Missus !"

He broke off abruptly, and hastened to open the door for his mistress ; who entered, according to her custom, as the great clock was striking the breakfast-hour.

CHAPTER IV.

No sooner were Mabel and her aunt fairly settled at breakfast, than the former, regardless of Thomas's warning, began her enquiries as to the missing picture.

It was impossible for her to rest with her curiosity ungratified; and this, she well knew, was her only chance for that day. Fräulein C., too thorough a foreigner to appreciate a sociable English breakfast-table, always took her cup of coffee and small roll in her own room. At dinner she would be with them; and, except at meals, Mrs. Stretton was rarely to be found disengaged.

"I am surprised that Thomas should have been speaking to you on family matters," said Mrs. Stretton, somewhat severely.

"Indeed, aunt," interposed Mabel, earnestly, "he never spoke to me about it at all. He only brought me an old list of the pictures, as I was trying to make them out; and when I saw the name of Sir Godfrey Kneller, I knew there was not one in the house by him; so I asked where it was now; and he said it had never been here in his time, and that I had better not ask about it."

"So you ask directly," said Mrs. Stretton. "Well, child, as the matter has taken hold of your curiosity, it is best to tell you the rights of it at once. Not that there is anything dishonourable to the family," she added, somewhat proudly, as she caught Mabel's intent, half-frightened look, "though it is a story we do not love to talk about. But," she continued, "you know that tablet in the church, to the memory of Richard Stretton, with the long list of sons; you remember the two eldest were twins?"

"Oh, yes!" said Mabel, "and I have often wondered what became of the eldest; I have never been able to find anything more about him, though I have looked at all the monuments and inscriptions."

"You would find nothing more about him at Ringwood," said Mrs. Stretton, somewhat mysteriously. "But, however, the twin brothers were brought up entirely together, and were strongly attached to each other, as twins usually are. The elder, as he grew old enough to understand his position, was indignant at being recognized as sole heir to the exclusion of his brother; they always, he said, had everything alike. He tried vehemently to induce his father to make a will, leaving the estate between them; but Mr. Stretton of course refused to dismember the property. He died some years before the boys were of age; after their education was finished, they both continued to live at Ringwood with their mother, declaring they would never separate. But as they had always been alike in all their tastes, both unhappily had the same fancy in the choice of a wife; and she whom they both loved, was a young cousin of their mother's. She was an orphan, with no settled home, and so was almost brought up at the Chace ; where she was the pet and pride of the whole house, and the darling of old Mr. and Mrs. Stretton, who had no daughter of their own."

" And was that her picture ? Was she very beautiful ?" asked Mabel, breathlessly.

" They say she was not exactly beautiful, only very charming," said Mrs. Stretton. " However, the old people were so proud of her, that they employed Sir Godfrey Kneller to take her portrait ; and this was considered one of the choicest treasures of the house. Well, in what way the three, or two of them, at least, came to understand how matters stood between them, no one ever seems to have known. The mother died before the two sons came of age, and Alice went to live with other relatives some way off. The one-and-twentieth birthday was celebrated with but moderate rejoicings, the family being still in mourning for their mother. The eldest son, however, entered into full possession. Shortly after, he started suddenly on a journey, telling no one whither he was going. Before long came a letter to his brother, inclosing a deed of gift, making over the property to him and to his heirs for ever; relinquishing all claim on the part of himself or any children he might have; reserving merely for his own maintenance the portion which he inherited of his mother's fortune. He was married, he went on to say, to Alice; was conscious that by this step he was destroying his brother's happiness; and that in ceding to him the estate, he was making a wholly inadequate reparation, having robbed him of what was so much more precious.

That he and Alice both felt they could never
bear to meet the brother whom they had so
bitterly wronged, although by no free-will of
their own ; that they meant to reside hence-
forth in seclusion, on a small farm which they
had purchased at a distance, and where they
entreated to be left undisturbed, only begging,
if even at some remote period, to be assured
of forgiveness.   The brother, as proud a
Stretton as ever was, wrote back at once, that
forgiveness was easily granted, the loss being
by no means so irreparable as they supposed.
He then sent to his brother the portrait,
which he said was now valueless to him.
And very soon after, he himself married ; but
had no children, and died before middlelife ;
both brothers, as sometimes occurs with
twins, dying on the same day, although living
far apart, and having no communication with
each other."

Mabel was sitting with wide-open eyes, and
a half-awed expression.

" And the poor wife ?" she asked.

" Alice ?   She seems to have died soon
after her husband ; and the children, if there
were any, to have strayed away somewhere
before any one thought of inquiring for
them."

" Aunt !" exclaimed Mabel, suddenly, her
whole face lighting up, " perhaps that was
how Edward and Clara came to be Strettons ;
and we may be cousins after all !"

" My dear Mabel ! what are you thinking
of ?"

" Why—you know they never could trace
farther back than—yes ;—let me see ;—yes,
the time, I suppose, might about correspond—
Oh, I am so glad ! I am so glad !"

" Mabel !" said her aunt, with more vehe-
mence than was usual with her, " I am surprised to hear you ! There is not the least
probability in the matter ; and if there were,
it is the last thing you ought to rejoice at."

" Oh, aunt ! I have so wished to belong to

them—to have them for relations, I mean," she added, correcting herself.

"My dear Mabel," said Mrs. Stretton, more quietly, "I know that they are excellent people, and have been very kind to you ; but they would not be suitable as relations. You do not understand these things. They belong to quite a different class of society."

"They are a great deal better than any of us, that is all I know !" said Mabel, warmly.

"You are quite right, Mabel, to speak so of such kind friends. I assure you I mean no disrespect towards them ; nothing was farther from my thoughts; in fact, I am deeply indebted——But you know relationship is quite a different matter. They have a place of business in the city, have they not?"

"The dear old place ! I love it !" said Mabel, audaciously.

Mrs. Stretton looked too much aghast to reply.

"Well," Mabel went on, "I will write to

Clara about it, and they will see what they can find out."

" Mabel! I beg you will not do anything so absurd !"

" I will!" said Mabel, shaking back her curls, and looking up at her aunt in half-laughing defiance.

Mrs. Stretton looked thunderstruck for a moment ; then she, in her turn, almost laughed.

" You self-willed little Stretton !" she said, patting the saucy head.

" You know, aunt, it is their right !"

" My dear Mabel, there is no right in the matter. Do you not remember my telling you that the elder son relinquished the inheritance for his *children*, as well as for himself; so, even supposing there was any truth in this absurd notion of yours, no pretensions to descent from *him* could give anyone the least claim to the estate."

" The estate !" exclaimed Mabel ; " I was

not thinking about the *estate;* they don't want *that.* But do you not think, aunt, that it is *something* to belong to the Strettons of Ringwood?"

Mrs. Stretton hesitated, rather at a loss what to reply.

"It is not easy to be angry with you, Mab," she said, with some complacency, after a moment's pause. But Mabel had fallen into one of her absent fits.

"Aunt," she said, suddenly starting up, "I have thought of something else!"

"My dear child, do be quiet! What have you in your head now?"

"I dare say, aunt, this was the picture they used to think like me;—I mean, which papa copied, because it was like mamma;—did I never tell you? It was at some farm-house. But then—I forgot—that lady was not a Stretton;—how should there be a likeness?" and Mabel stopped short, looking rather bewildered.

"She was a near relation, on the mother's side," said Mrs. Stretton; "so the likeness might come out in a later generation. Where was it, Mabel, my dear? I must send and make enquiries. At a farm-house, did you say? It would be a strange coincidence."

"I don't know where the farm-house was," said Mabel; "but I dare say it was the same. Where was the one they lived at, aunt? Who has it now? We can send and ask if they have a picture there."

"How provoking!" said Mrs. Stretton. "If you had only known the name of the place! That is what we have never been able to find out, or we should have enquired for the portrait long since. When the twin brothers died, a third brother came to the estate—(my grandfather)—quite a boy, who knew and cared nothing about the matter. And my father cared nothing either;—so the letters were all lost, and there is no clue left."

"Then, aunt," said Mabel, in despair, "what is the use? How are Clara and Edward to find out anything, if they don't know the place?"

"You see, my dear, it would be of no use," said Mrs. Stretton, forgetting her own disappointment, in her relief at the turn affairs had taken with respect to 'the Strettons.' "I am glad you are convinced."

"I must write to Clara, at all events," said Mabel; "and, oh! aunt, would you not like to see papa's copy of the portrait? Clara was only to take care of it for me till I wanted it. Would you not like to have it here till we can get back the real picture?"

This was no stroke of diplomacy on Mabel's part. Had it been so, it would have done credit to her skill. The inducement she held out was irresistible; that one suggestion did what no argument could have done; and it was not only with her aunt's consent, but at

her urgent desire, that she now wrote to
Clara; begging her to forward the portrait
with all convenient speed, and, of course, en-
larging fully on all the new notions now connected in her own mind therewith.

CHAPTER V.

MATTERS had subsided at Mr. Stretton's into that languid state which often supervenes when some great event is pending, but is hindered from immediate accomplishment by delays and obstacles over which the parties most deeply concerned have no direct power. Till the time of Aunt Sarah's joining them was definitely fixed, a certain doubt and hesitation hung over all preparations for the wedding; and compared with *that*, no other object seemed important enough to be worth much effort.

One point only was certain ; in three weeks would be Edward's one-and-twentieth birthday ; nothing could put that off; and on that day there must be a large party, for which invitations had already been issued ; and which was also to be, in fact, though not professedly, Clara's leave-taking to her friends. Aunt Sarah had promised to be with them in time for this party, if possible; her presence was much calculated on ; still, whether she were arrived or not, the party *must* take place. Yet the *tone* of the whole affair, and many minor details, would necessarily be much influenced by the length of the interval between this festival and Clara's marriage ; so that even about this one fixed point hovered the same doubtful haze of suspense and indecision.

One morning, when Clara had been wandering restlessly up and down, in a state of busy idleness, very different from her usual practical, unfaltering energy, the whim suddenly seized her of trying to copy Mabel's portrait, as she persisted in calling that in her morning-room. Mabel might send for it; very likely would send for it before long; and then how glad she should be to have a copy. So she had the picture brought down to the library, where her easel usually stood, and established herself at her work. Barlow had to remind her when it was time to dress for dinner; and when she was ready, instead of waiting, as usual, for her father and brother in the drawing-room, she passed again into the library, and settled herself to go on with her occupation till they should return. It was rather before their usual time; she had dressed quickly; and for some five or ten minutes she continued her drawing without interruption.

"Copying a copy, Clara?" said Dr. Harland's voice, close behind her.

She had not expected him down to dinner that day, and so engrossed was she with her employment, that he had been standing there for some minutes, watching her progress, without her perceiving it.

"By poor Arleigh, I suppose," he added; "and not badly done, either. The original must have been a very fine thing. Do you know where he came upon it, Clara? I should like a sight of it."

"Not in the least," said Clara; "Mabel always said that her father met with it at some old farm-house, but she did not know where. He copied it, thinking there was some likeness to his wife, else it is rather out of his line."

"A very pretty thing," said Dr. Harland, still looking at it. "But is it worth your while to copy it, Clara? It is generally better to draw from originals."

"We always thought it like our little Mab," said Clara; "that is why I want to have a copy, in case she should send for this, as I am always expecting she will. You hardly saw her, did you—not enough to judge of the likeness ?"

" Oh, yes, I saw her once or twice, plainly enough, though she was too shy ever to look at me. A nice little thing ; her face took my fancy ; and I was interested in her, when I learnt who she was, from what I had heard of poor Arleigh, so I took more notice of her than I might otherwise have done."

" And do you see any likeness ?" asked Clara.

" Why, yes, there really is something ; not the features so much, but a look of the eyes, which seem half smiling, while the general expression is thoughtful. But you have not caught *that*, Clara ; though otherwise your drawing is very promising, so far."

" No, I have not," said Clara ; " and I have been teasing myself about it all the morning, for it is in that, as you say, that the resemblance lies. Do alter it for me," she added, offering to put the pencil into his hand.

"Not I, indeed, Clara," said Dr. Harland, laughing; "you would repent if you once let me touch a drawing of yours. Have you not found out that I am a critic born?—That I can generally see what is amiss, but very rarely understand how to set it right?"

"I hope that does not hold good of your practice, Robert."

He turned round quickly, well pleased. Never before had she called him by his Christian name; scarcely ever had she bestowed on him one of her saucy speeches; never alluded with anything like playfulness to his profession, which always seemed a subject of peculiar annoyance to her. And all discussion of the portrait was for the time forgotten.

Then Mr. Stretton and Edward returned; then dinner was announced; then the afternoon post came in; and by one of those odd coincidences which are constantly occurring, yet which never fail to strike us as strange and exceptional whenever they do occur, this post brought Mabel's letter respecting the portrait so recently under discussion. But it brought also a letter far more interesting in the actual juncture of affairs. Aunt Sarah would join them on the eve of Edward's birthday.

"It seems cruel of me, dear Clara," she wrote, " to have kept you all so long in uncertainty, and now to come to you so late as to be of little use in the preparations you must have to make. But the business which has detained me has been so lingering and uncertain, that I could neither control nor foresee the exact period of its accomplishment ; and *at last* have only settled the matter by fixing the latest possible day for my departure, and determining, when that arrives, to leave all behind me, finished or unfinished."

Poor little Mabel ! everything conspired to make *her* letter fall flat. It was at first laid aside with a quiet " Oh ! from Mabel," and quite forgotten for a considerable time, while

F 2

the immediate arrangements and plans result-
ing from the other were discussed; then,
when Clara at length bethought her to open
it, she indeed exclaimed, "How odd! Mabel
has really sent for the picture! so I had a
true presentiment." But Dr. Harland, to
whom this was addressed, knew nothing of
the principal subject on which the letter
turned; and it was impossible to explain anything so elaborate to him just then, in the
midst of matters so much more engrossing.
So Clara merely handed the letter to her
father, who cared for points of ancestry or
genealogical questions not at all; and first
glancing hastily through it, to be satisfied
that the child was well and happy, was giving
it back to Clara, with merely an acknowledging nod, when Edward stretched out his
hand for it.

"You have no objection, I suppose, Clara?"
said Mr. Stretton, as he gave up the letter.

Clara merely nodded in her turn; she

was listening to something which Dr. Harland, in a low, earnest voice, was saying to her.

Edward read it through with attention; even turning back once or twice to refer to what had gone before; and was about to make some remark, as he at last handed it to his sister; but seeing her preoccupied face, he checked himself, and joined in the general conversation.

Clara, however, never forgot any practical piece of business entrusted to her, nor ever executed any in a negligent manner. Accordingly, when Edward was leaving the breakfast-table next morning, she concluded a long list of commissions which she had been giving him, with—

"And oh, Edward, would you be so good as to make arrangements about Mabel's picture? We ought to have it packed by some one accustomed to such things, that it may not be injured by the way; will you inquire for a proper person, and settle how it had best be sent?"

And now Clara's life was turned into a state of siege; her quiet, hitherto impregnable morning-room overrun by invading dress-makers and milliners, and not unfrequently hung with gaily-coloured trophies of their successful incursions. She had, it must be confessed, some compensating enjoyment, in the midst of the incessant worry; for she had a true woman's pleasure in such matters, an innate love and instinct for dress, which could not fairly be called vanity; for her own looks occupied but little of her attention; and though by no means deficient in self-appreciation, she hardly knew how handsome she really was. But elegance,—perhaps splendour,—was her prevailing taste in all things; she loved them for her own enjoyment therein, far more than for any impression connected with herself which might be made on others. With regard to dress, she forgot her own from the moment when she left her glass; but sometimes, even in mixed society, it seemed difficult for her to refrain from crossing the room, to remonstrate with some entire stranger, whose attire happened to offend her eye, as inappropriate or unbecoming.

And those maternal duties, from which she had at first professed to shrink in horror, she had already in some part taken on herself; having the two children almost constantly with her, on the plea that she could not trust their old nurse to superintend the making of their new frocks.

Little Janet, the elder, now about seven, enjoyed the business fully as much as her step-mamma elect. She was rather a taking-looking child, though pale and puny; her delicate little features, white skin, and animated eyes, partially compensating for the want of childish bloom and roundness. And little Missy, as she was familiarly called, knew full well already how to make the most of such advantages as she did possess; and appreciated at even more than their due value her own tiny foot and fairy-like figure. Bating this little bit of vanity, a good child enough; very easily won by kindness, though not very deep in any of her feelings.

Annie, the younger, was rather plain, rather sickly, and rather cross; distinguished chiefly by a painful, morbid sensitiveness; which Janet made fun of, the servants scolded at, and her father sometimes cheerily put aside, sometimes looked at rather anxiously, as a medical symptom: in which he was, perhaps, not very far wrong.

"How do I look?" said Janet, dancing into the morning-room, dressed in the important frock which was to be worn at both the party and the wedding, and which the dress-maker had just been trying on.

"Very pretty indeed," said Clara, absently, only just lifting her eyes from the note she was writing.

"Oh no, not *pretty* ; Nurse says that little girls never *are* pretty," replied Janet, hastily.

"Nurse is quite right, I dare say," said Clara; "I was not thinking of what I was saying. But your frock does very nicely, dear, at any rate."

"And if Mr. Stretton or Mr. Edward should ask, 'What is little Janet going to wear?'—you can tell them I have a pretty new frock; and if they ask how I look in it,—you can tell them what you think," said Janet, hanging her head bashfully.

"You little coquette!" exclaimed Clara, laughing.

"What is that? is it something ugly?—Oh, tell me!" said Janet in dismay; running to the chimney-glass, and looking herself anxiously over.

"Don't be frightened, Missy; you will do very well. Now give me a kiss;" and the child, clasping her arms about Clara's neck, half stifled her with caresses; calling her her dear, beautiful, charming new mamma. She had persisted in giving her by anticipation the title which she had been told she was to bear.

Annie, meanwhile, had had her frock tried on, in listless silence.

"Won't you go, dear, and show Miss Stretton your pretty new frock, as your sister has done?" had been nurse's suggestion.

"No, I won't!" said Annie, doggedly; and she stood in sullen silence till the dress had been taken off, and the dressmaker departed.

"What makes you so cross, Miss Annie?" enquired nurse, at length.

"I am not cross."

"Why wouldn't you go and show your pretty frock?"

"Betsy"—(the nursery-maid)—"says I ought to love my new mamma. I can't love her because I *ought*."

"*Ought*, Miss Annie? who ever heard of such a thing? I wonder what Betsy means, talking such nonsense! *Ought*, indeed!—As if anyone was obliged to love a step-mother; who will be cross and cruel enough, no doubt, as they all are."

" Then you think," pursued Annie, " she won't love *me*?"

" Love *you*, poor innocent! take my word for it, all the love she has to spare will be for Miss Janet, just because she is pretty and fondling-like. Why, isn't she all taken up with her already? No, my darling, nobody loves *you*, or is like to, but your poor old nurse."

" And I need not love her unless I like?"

" Not a bit of it!—And I promise you, it's little love she'll get from any of us. We've all made up our minds to hate her."

Annie made no reply. But the next time she found herself alone with Clara, she crept up close beside her, and slid her little hand into hers. Nurse's intemperate heat had injured her own cause. Something in the child's nature made it easier to her to give her love as a freewill offering; and something, also, inclined her to take part with one whom she heard threatened with that general dislike which her morbid fancy had imagined her own portion.

Clara, fortunately perhaps for all parties, was far from fully understanding Annie's very peculiar and somewhat unhealthy temperament. But she was entirely kind-hearted, and really pitied the wan, heavy-eyed little girl, whose questioning, doubting gaze she was perpetually meeting. She decidedly felt her more interesting than Janet; and her genuine kindness, and slight preference, were before long answered on Annie's part by a depth of passionate attachment such as the child had never before felt for any one, and never, while childhood lasted, felt for any other.

But Clara's attention was by no means engrossed with these new and personal interests. She had an unavowed impression that the

comforts of those she was leaving *must* suffer
in any hands but her own ; and after regu-
lating all household matters to the highest
point of finish, she exhausted herself in endless
instructions and injunctions to old nurse, upon
whom she relied for initiating her aunt into
the family ways.

And, in the midst of all this, the birthday
party had to be organized. And a great
blessing it was; something to organize was
the delight of Clara's heart; and thoroughly
did she enjoy this, her last act of home queen-
ship, which had also the pleasant feeling of
being for Edward, so much more than for
herself.

But the picture was duly packed and sent,
and Clara found time to write the following
hurried note to Mabel :—

"Thank you, my dear, darling Mabel, for
your long letter, and yet more for still retaining the wish to have us for cousins.
Cousins we may be, Mab dear; but the dis-

covery is not made yet. I wish very sincerely that we could trace out the clue you suggest; but, as you know, we have already tried in vain to learn where our great-grandfather came from; and as you cannot tell us the name of the village where the farm-house you refer to was situated, I do not see that we can do anything further in the matter. The story sounds rather improbable, and very likely has been handed down with embellishments, as such family histories often are.

"I am so busy, I hardly know what I write; however, I will forward the portrait directly, as you wish. I had begun to copy it for your sake, but I think I remember you well enough to do without a likeness. The picture will be directed to the Chace; but as the coach goes no farther than N——, the package will be forwarded thence by carrier, unless Mrs. Stretton thinks proper to make any special arrangement as to its conveyance.

"Next Thursday week, when Edward, you

know, will be one-and-twenty, we are to have
a large party; you will think of us then. The
boys are to come home in time for it. And
the next week, I shall want you, my little
Mabel, oh, so much! But it is no use, I can't
have you, I know. The two little girls are to
be my bridesmaids; they will wear pink crape
frocks; they are so pleased, poor little things!
The elder, Janet, is really rather pretty, and
they will both look very well when they are
properly dressed. They have no one now to
see to them but their nurse, who, of course,
does not understand such things.

" Good-bye, dear Mab ;—no, not good-bye
—I hate that word. You know that I shall
be always, just the same,

" Your loving

" CLARA."

CHAPTER VI.

AFFECTIONATE as Clara's letter was, Mabel read it through with a blank expression of face, and a strong inclination to cry. Her own vague conjectures had become to *her* mind such established facts, that the possibility had never occurred to her of their being viewed as improbabilities; in the extreme quiet, the unbroken monotony of her daily life, the affair had assumed such disproportionate importance, that to have it treated as something quite subordinate to the engrossing realities of the hour was almost more than she could bear. She was bitterly mortified.

She had fought the battle so valiantly and successfully, in overcoming her aunt's objections ; she had so calculated upon the interest, the excitement, which her history would occasion ; she had so rejoiced in being able, for the first time as she thought, to give pleasure, perhaps to render real service, to her early friends.

" I thought at least that they would have cared more about having me for a relation ! To be sure Clara *must* be too busy for anything ;—but Edward ! And yet, if they are going to lose *her*, it is no wonder they can think of nothing else."

Rising abruptly, she went out upon the north terrace, and walked hurriedly up and down. Her throat swelled, her cheeks were flushed, her lips trembled, she could scarcely keep down her tears. The fresh north air blew the hair from her forehead, and somewhat cooled her cheeks ; the choking feeling grew less.

" What nonsense! how absurd I am!" she murmured half aloud. " I will go and see Catherine," was her next thought, and, turning suddenly back into the house, she ran upstairs.

At one of the sharp turns in the gallery she came full upon her aunt.

" Please, aunt, may I go and see Catherine this morning ?"

" Yes, to be sure, Mabel ; but mind to be home in time for dinner. Had you not better wait, and go in the afternoon ?—you would not be so hurried."

" Oh, no, please, aunt! I would rather go now," said Mabel, with difficulty, and hurrying by her; for the kept-back tears were now falling like rain.

" Very well, then, run away," said Mrs. Stretton, who had perceived nothing; and Mabel, hastily tying on her bonnet, ran down stairs again, and out into the park.

The air was so buoyant, the sunshine,

glancing between the boughs, and wavering in network meshes on the turf, was so pleasant, that by the time she had reached Calder House she had almost forgotten her vexation.

"Why, what is the matter with you, Mab, dear?" were Catherine's first words.

It was now Mabel's turn to be reserved.

"Nothing, Catherine, except nonsense," she said, blushing deeply.

The brave little heart could not complain of one friend to another.

"I want to see how the conservatory is going on," she added, hastily.

Catherine threw a timid, doubtful glance at her friend, and then silently led the way to the conservatory.

In a forlorn-looking plight they found it— the ground ploughed up by the wheels of the carts employed in the work; the plaster scraped off the front, and scattered all around; the floor of the saloon taken up for

the needful repairs of the fountain-pipes ; the
creepers turned back from the roof, and lying
in tangled masses amid the slough.

But to the eyes of the two girlish " sur-
veyors," the place already wore the aspect
which it was eventually to assume; and they
were soon deep in anticipations of luxurious
winter lounges amid the flowers and fragrance
of warmer climes ; of long summer noontides
in the bowery little saloon, freshened by the
plashings of the fountain. They were even
planning a Midsummer breakfast there, of
strawberries and cream, in Arthur's especial
honour, and which Frank, nay, even Mrs.
Stretton, must be beguiled to join.

" How different everything seems since
you came to Ringwood!" said Catherine,
putting her arm affectionately round Mabel's
waist. " Before that, I scarcely used to take
pleasure in anything. And Frank—I suppose
he is altered, too, in some way; for I am
hardly ever afraid of him now. I often

wonder, when I think how short a time it really is since you came ; you seem to *belong* here ; and I can scarcely help fancying you must have been here always, and that we never could have gone on without you. And then, sometimes, I am half frightened lest you should vanish as suddenly as you appeared. For you have an odd look and way with you, Mab ; not quite 'canny,' as my old Scotch nurse used to say. I must chain you tight, or you will be off, and we may never catch you again."

And in a mood of unwonted playfulness, Catherine snatched up the long snapped-off tendrils of some heavy-leaved creeping plant, broken by the reckless workmen, and twined them tightly round and round Mabel, pretending to imprison even her hands in the long flexible coils, and twisting them round her throat and waist.

Catherine was in unusual spirits at the progress of her works, and at the prospect of her brother's surprise and pleasure when he should return, and find them completed. For the moment she was as frolicsome as Mabel herself.

But when she paused, and looked at the mock captive, who stood with folded hands and bowed head, in feigned submission, before her, she first laughed, then shook her head.

"It is no use, Mab! I can see your eyes, and the wicked look in them, though you do cast them down! I might as well try to bind that saucy little brook! You look more like a real Queen Mab than ever, with all those green leaves about you. I should not be surprised if this very minute my chains gave way, and you were off in a nutshell. And oh! I am so tired!" And Catherine, quite exhausted with her unwonted game of romps, flung herself down upon one of the old stone dolphins which the workmen had removed from the brink of the fountain, and left lying about. It was the only available seat, in the present state of the building.

" Why, Catherine, you look like a mermaid ! Surely I have a right to call names, as well as you !" exclaimed Mabel, as Catherine threw down her bonnet, loosened in her sport, and her comb fell to the ground, setting free the hair, which had been gathered up in one great coil at the back of her head, and which now fell in profuse waves over her whole figure.

Catherine's hair had no natural curl, like Mabel's ; but instead, the extreme and silky softness peculiar to redundant fair hair.

" Why, that is the very thing ! Your hair would float and swell upon the waves, like the seaweed we used to see, heaving and swaying on the sea, in dear old Wales ! Beautiful old Wales ! I wish I could see it again !" and Mabel half sighed. " Oh, see, Catherine ! here is a looking-glass for you !" as she picked up one of the broken fragments of glass, left from the ruin of the old conservatory. "Now you will be quite complete! There! hold it so!" placing it in her hand. "And your comb too! Oh, Catherine! if you could only sing!

—' A mermaid, sitting on a dolphin's back,'—

you know, and so on!"

"What is the use of teasing me about that, you wicked little Mab, when you know I *can't*. Only listen!" and leaning back on the old stone dolphin, she began a low, monotonous chant, certainly not unsuitable to the character which Mabel had assigned to her—something like the murmuring of a seashell, or the wailing of the ocean-waves,—but by no stretch of language to be dignified with the name of *singing*.

Suddenly she started up, and in great trepidation and confusion, gathered up her hair and arranged her bonnet, as she perceived the workpeople beginning to return from their dinner.

" Oh, Catherine, what o'clock is it?" exclaimed Mabel, in alarm.

Catherine consulted the pretty little watch at her side (Mabel had no watch as yet).

"It wants just ten minutes to two, Mabel, dear; you may be in time, if you run."

And Mabel *did* run ; just controlling her eager steps while she traversed the few yards of public road between Calder House gates and the little wicket door in the palings of the Chace ; but when she had passed the latter, darting on afresh, startling the birds among the branches, and the dappled deer couched around the great tree boles, while a confused whirr of heavy wings, and a hoarse, indignant caw broke from the great rookery, as she passed one end of an old elm grove.

Panting and breathless she reached the ever-open door, passed swiftly across the hall,

and sprang up the stairs. She was received
at the door of her own room by Bianca, who
was standing there in a tragic attitude of
terror and suspense, changing instantly, when
she caught sight of Mabel, to rapid gestures
of warning and exhortation, as she drew her
young mistress quickly into the room, where
she had long since completed every possible
preparation for a hurried toilet. She was
expert in such emergencies; and no wonder—
Mabel's unpunctual habits gave her full practice.

Not a word did Bianca utter, until, by one
magic touch as it seemed, the bright hair
had been restored to some degree of smooth-
ness,—until the pretty lilac muslin dress had
replaced the little morning frock of striped
pink gingham. Then, with a sweeping wave
of one hand, as she held the door wide open
with the other, she pronounced—

" There is time yet, Signorina."

And the dinner-bell rang, as Mabel, jumping down the last three steps of the staircase, met her aunt crossing the hall to the dining-room.

Once again she was safe. She had escaped what she most dreaded on earth, the brief, stern rebuke from one whom she loved well enough to make her displeasure a torture, and not quite well enough to cast out fear.

CHAPTER VII.

Was ever anything so provoking?—Catherine was standing with such calm satisfaction among her works, receiving the workmen's reassuring promises that all would be beautiful by the time the master came home; when the said master, unexpected, unannounced, himself appeared upon the scene.

Catherine stood for one moment the picture of shame and despair, like one caught in the commission of some guilty deed; then, seeming to recollect herself, she rallied her courage by a sudden effort, and stepped forward to meet her brother.

"Dear Frank, I hoped this would all be finished by the time you came home—I wanted to surprise you."

"My dear Catherine, I am so glad—at least, I am sorry if I have spoiled your pleasure—but it is such a good notion of yours; and now we can finish it together."

"Dear Frank! I thought—I hoped it would please you; Mabel said she was sure it would."

"Then it was Miss Arleigh who put it into your head?" said Frank, looking half pleased, half disappointed.

"No, indeed, it was all my own plan; only Mabel had been saying she wondered I did not order things as you always wished me; and how she should enjoy it if she—that is— she meant, I know, what a kind brother I have," said Catherine, the tears, in spite of herself, rising into her deep blue eyes.

"She was quite right," said Frank, taking his sister's hand affectionately. "I mean," he added, colouring and laughing, "quite right in teaching you to have a will of your own. But now, Cathie, dear," he continued, "do you think the men could go on for a week or two without our looking after them? I came back in a hurry, because I found I had a little spare time; and I wanted to take you with me for a little journey, if you would like it?"

Catherine's eyes absolutely glittered.

"Oh, Frank! how very kind! And no one with us?"

"Hannah will go with you, of course."

"And my cousin?"

"That can be just as you like," said Frank, looking rather searchingly at his sister.

"She would like to go, would she not?"

"I do not think she would care much, either way. She has had an invitation to visit one of her nieces, which I think she would like just as well, unless you would rather she went with us."

"Oh, then, dear Frank, pray do let us go all alone together. It will be so pleasant, only our two selves."

Frank looked greatly pleased.

"I thought you would not be afraid to go with me alone, Catherine," he said.

This was very ill judged, and might have spoilt the whole, by frightening her again. But she was in a courageous mood, and only asked cheerfully—

"And when are we to go?"

"Can you be ready to-morrow morning?"

"Oh, to be sure. I will go and tell Hannah. Only," she added, turning back, "I must bid Mabel good-bye this evening."

"Of course; we will walk up there together after dinner."

"And then," said Catherine, "I will ask her to come here sometimes, and see that all goes on rightly at the conservatory while I am away."

That afternoon, while the brother and sister were walking across the park, Fräulein C. and Mabel were, according to custom, alone in the library; Mabel sitting unusually still, and working with unusual steadiness at the wedding gift, the embroidered pocket-hand-kerchief. Something had gone wrong in the pattern; the work had in consequence been despairingly thrown aside, and all progress suspended for a longer interval than usual. This afternoon, however, Mabel's brows were resolutely bent, as she sat for some time silent and intent, trying to set herself right.

"What is it, my child?" asked Fräulein C. at last.

Mabel, rising with a reluctant sigh, gave the work into her hand. Fräulein C. pondered over it, as a physician ponders over a difficult case. At length she shook her head.

"It is *no go*," she said, slowly and reluctantly; unwittingly anticipating a slang phrase of later date, in her conscientious effort to render every idiom by its equivalent.

"It *must* do," said Mabel, " or I must begin another."

"Well, well, we will see," said the Fräulein, soothingly; and after half an hour's tedious diligence, the unlucky embroidery was once more in order.

With one deep-breathed "Thank you!" Mabel took it from her, and withdrawing to her corner, was soon as deeply engrossed as ever; while Fräulein C. placidly took up the knitting which she had laid down, and resumed the task with unruffled composure.

At this juncture Thomas slowly and half doubtingly opened the door, announcing Mr. and Miss Calder. Visitors were so rare, that he hardly knew whether he was doing right.

Mabel had put back her long curls behind her ears, that the shadow might not fall upon her work; her eyes, as she slowly, almost reluctantly, raised them, had an anxious, pre-occupied expression, and seemed quite heavy with her intent poring. She looked paler, graver, almost *taller* than usual; and received the two unexpected visitors with something like shyness.

"My aunt will be here directly," she said, half apologetically; while Catherine pressed forward for the usual kiss; retaining Mabel's hand, and disregarding all Fräulein C.'s polite offers of a seat.

"We are come to say good-bye, Mabel; Frank is going to take me a journey with him. Is it not nice? And you will walk over sometimes, won't you? to see how the conservatory is going on—and that the men do all rightly, just as we planned? There is nobody else who knows about it.—Why, dear Mab!"—and by an instinctive impulse she drew her aside, for poor Mabel was struggling with her tears. Her morning's disappointment, her hurried walk home, and subsequent anxious poring over her work, had lowered her usually buoyant tone of spirits ; and the sudden announcement, that Catherine was going away—that she was, as she felt at the moment, to be left alone—came upon her with almost a sense of desolation.

" Well, Catherine," said Frank, coming up, " have you persuaded Miss Arleigh to play overseer for us ?"

He looked surprised, as he caught sight of Mabel's face ; but in a moment she had nearly recovered herself, and said, in a steady, though low voice :—

" I am so glad that Catherine is going with you !"

Just then Mrs. Stretton entered the room ; and Frank, after a moment's hesitation, and a questioning look at the two girls, went forward to shake hands with her, and explain. He had brought his sister, he said, to take leave for a little time ; she was going from home with him.

Mrs. Stretton looked almost too much startled to make any appropriate reply. She shook hands graciously with Catherine, who then sat down in her usual silent way; Mabel sitting silent beside her, and keeping her eyes fixed on the floor, with a look half resolute, half ashamed.

"And where do you think of going?" Mrs. Stretton enquired of Frank.

"Oh! Cathie and I shall start out like two knights-errant on our adventures, shall we not, Catherine?—go on till we come to a place where three roads meet—and then take our chance for what fortune will send us."

Mabel looked up with an amused smile; and presently, while Frank kept up the conversation with Mrs. Stretton, she was talking eagerly with Catherine, making suggestions, and asking questions; her cheek glowing, and her eyes sparkling. After a little time, he suddenly rose, reminded Catherine that she had a great deal to do, apologized to Mrs.

Stretton, shook hands with Mabel, and hurried his sister away; only giving the girls time for a hasty kiss, and leaving Mabel rather bewildered, but still bright and smiling, and altogether too much taken by surprise to realize the pain of parting.

The separation, indeed, of a few weeks was a little thing, scarcely worth grieving about; only the extreme isolation and monotony of her life gave it undue importance in her eyes.

*　　*　　*　　*　　*

A few days afterwards, as Mabel, according to custom, was leaving the school-room about noon, she was met by old Thomas, who told her that her aunt wanted her in her business-room. Thither she accordingly hurried; her knock receiving no answer, she rather timidly opened the door, and was startled by seeing the well-remembered picture, before which Mrs. Stretton was standing, rapt and absorbed.

"It *is* like poor Margaret," she at length murmured; the words seeming to escape her nvoluntarily.

"I am so glad, aunt!" said Mabel, fervently.

"You there, child? I had forgotten you." But she put her arm round Mabel's waist, and drew her forward with far more tenderness than usual, still gazing intently on the portrait. Then she looked from the picture to Mabel, putting back her hair, and examining her face intently.

"You have not the shadow of your mother in you," was her final judgment, accompanied by a half-stifled sigh. And, in fact, under this close comparison, and the constraint of scrutiny, Mabel scarcely resembled the portrait at all. "There will never be such another! Would you like to have this picture in your own room, my dear?"

"Oh! aunt, if you are so very kind! do *you* not want it?"

"That is its fit place, dear; where *she* would have wished to be."

"If we find the original," said Mabel, timidly, "perhaps you will like to have that."

"The original?" said Mrs. Stretton, looking for a moment quite bewildered; then, quickly recollecting herself—"I had forgotten all about that story; I was thinking it was Margaret's own portrait."

CHAPTER VIII.

The breakfast-table was a merry one at Mr. Stretton's on the morning of Edward's much-talked-of birthday.   It was laid out with rather extra profusion—not in the dining-room, as usual—but in a large, half-furnished, nondescript room, on the opposite side of the hall, formerly the boys' playroom ; though they now were beginning to despise the notion, and scorned to be drafted off into a sort of honourable banishment, whenever a wet day confined them to the house.

From an early hour this morning, the

dining and drawing-rooms had been in a state
of chaos, which had resulted in their being
before breakfast-time completely cleared, in
preparation for the dances. The library, with
the pretty little bowery greenhouse into which
it opened, was to remain undisturbed, a refuge
for the idle or the weary; and therein the
choicest treasures of the house had been concentrated, till it looked· like a fairy casket.
So the playroom alone remained available for
family occupation; and studiously as the boys
ignored its normal purposes, they felt somewhat bound to do the honours of the apartment. They had worked hard the preceding
day, decorating the walls with gigantic fes-
toons of evergreen; and the table now displayed an immense central nosegay, of asters,
marigolds, and all the gaudiest autumnal
flowers, to greet Edward when he came down
to breakfast. And Edward, still feeling, and
even looking, a good deal of a boy himself,
despite his honours of majority, laughed, co-

loured, and shrugged his shoulders, as he submitted to be almost pulled down by his
brothers' boisterous greeting—to be kissed,
rather more warmly than he thought necessary, by his sister—shaken hands with by his
father and aunt, bowed and curtsied to by
the servants—and bewildered by the general
influx of gifts and congratulations.

Nurse, a privileged person, pressed forward,
after the other servants had withdrawn.

"This is a proud day for us all, Master Edward, sir—I beg pardon, Mr.—"

"Never mind, it is all right," said Edward,
goodnaturedly, shaking the old woman cordially by the hand as he spoke.

"And may you live, sir, many happy years,
and be as good a man as your papa, sir, and
bring home as good a wife as your poor dear
mamma; God bless her for a good, kind
lady!"

Edward turned suddenly round again to
the speaker (his attention had wandered a

little when the speech was beginning) ; and
with a half-boyish impulse, part feeling, part
fun, in great part to cover a sensation of em-
barrassment, he cut the old lady's eloquence
short with a hearty kiss, such as he used to
give her when he came home, in jacket and
outgrown trowsers, for the holidays.

The old woman bridled and coloured, as if
she had been sixteen instead of sixty.

" Oh, Master Edward, you was always full
of your tricks !"

" I am ashamed to hear you utter such
calumnies, nurse ! You know very well I was
the best child you ever had to do with ! But
it is so long ago, you have forgotten ; you are
confounding me with Fred !"

Be it observed, that the said young gentleman, a genius in his own line, had just left
the room, to superintend some especial and
secret devices of his invention, in the way of
blue and other coloured lights, by which
he proposed to vary the amusements of

the evening, and terrify or delight the guests.

"Oh, well, sir, Master Fred may be a little *rusty* (restive) now and then—but I have nothing to say against any of my children. I have lived in many families, the best of families, sir"—(to Mr. Stretton)—"and never met better children than our children." And nurse curtsied herself out of the room.

When breakfast was over, the party adjourned to a side-table, whereon were displayed such of the birthday gifts as could be so exhibited. While the general buzz of inspection and admiration was going on, Aunt Sarah noiselessly left the room; and as noiselessly returned, carrying in her hand a small, flat packet, which she brought to the table and quietly opened; too quietly for the boys' impatient curiosity.

"I had hoped to give you really an agreeable surprise for your birthday, Edward, but

I have been disappointed. Yet you will value this, I know."

It was the favourite old copy of the Stretton shield and crest; old Hugh Stretton's school boy performance—the sole memorial of his origin which he had handed down to his children.

Edward seized it gratefully.

"Is it really for me, Aunt Sarah? You could not have given anything else so acceptable. I have wanted it ever since I remember."

"At all events, you see its value is now increased; only you must not be disappointed," said Aunt Sarah, with some hesitation, turning upwards the back, on which appeared, in scrawling schoolboy letters, the inscription:

"HUGH STRETTON.

HOLMFIRTH."

"Father! Clara! Look! Come here!— We have found what we wanted!"

" No, Edward! it is a false hope ; at least, I can gain no tidings of such a place."

Edward looked blank.

" I wanted," said his aunt, "to have the frame newly burnished, to make the thing fit for a birthday gift ; and the false paper back being removed, this inscription appeared. Then I thought that I had only to enquire for the place, and that I should be able to surprise you with the information you wished, or perhaps with something still more valuable. So first I quietly looked in the map ; looked patiently through the whole set of England in counties ;—no such name could I discover. Then I took down a Gazetteer; then the Encyclopædia ;—no better luck."

" How provoking!" said Clara ; "it must be some very small place."

" I hardly think that," said Aunt Sarah. " I remember my father used rather to pique himself on the boast that *his* father, though he rose from a poor boy, was not uneducated ;

having had very fair teaching before he came up to London, in the endowed school of his native *town.*—You can imagine father boasting of this,"—she added, turning to her brother;—" piquing himself on the education, and also glorying in making no secret that it had been gratuitous."

" Oh," said Edward, " it is just like him. Can you not see him, Clara, with his powdered hair and his silver buckles? I can fancy I hear him saying it."

" I have been making enquiries far and wide ; putting learned and unlearned on the quest," pursued Aunt Sarah ; " but so far, there is not a glimmer of hope."

" Write to Mabel about it," said Mr. Stretton, who had hitherto taken no part in the conversation. " Set her sharp little wits to work ; she will be delighted."

" Yes, poor child ! how proud she will be," said Clara. " And there can be no awkwardness, as Mrs. Stretton is so anxious to discover the place."

"You are taking for granted that it *is* the place," said Edward, laughing.

"Of course!" said Clara; "we are sure of that."

"After all," said Edward, "I don't see what good the poor child can do. She can learn nothing but what is known at Ringwood; and that she has told us already."

"I have faith in Mabel," said Mr. Stretton; "if it is to be found out, she will find it,— But after all, what does it matter to us?"

"You are talking riddles to me," said Aunt Sarah.

"Oh, I forgot," said Clara; "you have not heard about it. I must show you Mabel's last letter."

But at this moment a tap at the door mysteriously summoned Clara to give some directions respecting preparations for the evening.

"You can explain to your aunt, Edward," said Mr. Stretton, also preparing to leave the

room. "And you had better write to Mabel
yourself," he added, turning back, when half
outside the door. "Your sister will have
plenty to do."

And so the matter rested; and, in fact,
was soon well-nigh forgotten. For just as
Edward was beginning, for his aunt's benefit,
a brief abstract of Mabel's last communication,
and of the conjectures and speculations
founded thereon, he was interrupted by the
entrance of a servant bearing a waiter literally
heaped with letters : congratulatory birth-day
letters ;—letters of which one knows the contents before opening them; yet which it is
impossible to resist opening instantly, and
reading straight through, every word, before
moving from the spot. There is something so
comfortable in the certainty that in not one of
those overflowing letters will be found even
the shadow of aught unpleasant. And when
the perusal was completed, it was time for
him to start for London. Not even on that

day, it appeared, could the daily observance
be omitted.   It might be that some important business really rendered his attendance
that day essential at the counting-house; or,
possibly, he might think it too like a boy—a
school-boy—to make holiday on the strength
of his birth-day, even the one-and-twentieth!
He might have a lurking dread of some good-
humoured bantering from his father; might
shrink from placing himself in any respect on
a footing with John and Fred, and thus afford-
ing those saucy rogues some licence, of which
they would only too readily avail themselves,
for taking liberties.   He had still enough of
the boy in him to dislike especially being
thought such.   However this may have
been, he departed manfully to London that
day, and Aunt Sarah remained unenlightened.
Indeed, it is doubtful whether she would
herself have had leisure to attend to him;
only that she was one of those wonderful
persons who can attend to anybody, in

the midst of anything, without hurry or disturbance.

Mr. Stretton's household arrangements
were by no means on so distinguished a footing that a large party could be given without a tolerable amount of previous disturbance,
and at least one day's absorbing attention on
the part of Clara herself. But Aunt Sarah
seemed made for emergencies. Noiselessly
and unobtrusively she glided from room to
room, from the upper to the lower regions;
ready at any moment to suggest, to approve,—
to give a casting vote where there had seemed
no hope of arriving at a decision; appearing
always, by some happy magic, just when and
where she was wanted; and all with such
intuitive and delicate tact, that it was impossible for the young mistress of the house to
fancy herself for one moment superseded, before the time, by her chosen successor.

Just as Clara's toilet was completing that
evening, a tap was heard at the door.

" Come in, nurse. Thank you, Barlow, that will do very nicely now, I think."

She knew the tap and the errand. Since Clara had outgrown nurse's hair-dressing skill, the old woman had been deposed from her office of attendant on her young mistress; but the affair had been managed with great tact, so that she still 'regarded herself as the responsible person, and Barlow merely as a deputy; and felt it both her duty and her privilege to *look* Clara thoroughly *over* on all important occasions, before she left her chamber, to see that nothing was amiss.

Barlow, upon due representation of the circumstances, submitted to this imaginary supervision; but she could hardly be expected to do so with a very good grace. Besides, she was really jealous of nurse, and with some cause; Clara naturally loved and confided in the old attendant of her childhood, as only an attendant of childhood *can* be loved and trusted. So a certain hostility was always smouldering between the parties, though in general decently suppressed.

"Well, you do look charming to-night, Miss Clara, to be sure!"

"Your gloves, ma'am," said Barlow, officiously interposing.

"Thank you, Barlow; that will do now."

"Your fan, ma'am."

"Thank you. Just go and see how the lamps are burning; I shall be down directly."

"Your bouquet, ma'am; Gibson hoped you would approve of it."

"Oh, it is charming!" she exclaimed, and she half buried her face in the odorous, glowing mass of bloom. "And now I think of it, some of those plants want arranging. Go and talk to Gibson about it."

And Barlow was at length happily dismissed.

"Well!" nurse again began, "you do look charming, Miss Clara, this evening!"

Nurse was quite right. The delicate pearl

spray set off admirably Clara's masses of glossy black hair, and her undulating figure showed to the best advantage in its clouds of white drapery.

"And I know who will think so, too," pursued the old woman.

But the heightened colour, and sudden change of expression, showed that, even from *her*, no remarks would be tolerated on that point.

"And little Miss Mabel," said nurse, dexterously changing the subject, "how proud and pleased she would have been to see you!"

"I wish she were here, poor child," said Clara, with a half-sigh.

"Perhaps, ma'am, we may have her here again before very long. I should not wonder if Mr. Edward—"

"Nonsense, nurse! nothing of the kind. *That* can never be, I knew that all along; and *now!* Pray do not let me hear a word more on the subject."

" Oh, well, ma'am, and I daresay it's no great loss ; she was always a half-wild, odd sort of child ; one never knew where to have her ; and Mr. Edward, that might have the pick of the country ; plenty a deal prettier, and richer too; —though she may hold up her head now for a great lady, since she is at Ringwood Chace."

Nurse was particularly unlucky in her subjects. Clara could neither endure to hear Mabel depreciated, nor to have her spoken of as in any possible sense superior to Edward in worldly position. She could hardly command her irritation.

" Nurse, I wish you would just look to the curtains down-stairs, and see that there are no draughts to give people cold. There is no one I can depend on but you."

" Ah, to be sure, ma'am, there's a many catches their death of cold in a ball-room !" and with this cheerful suggestion nurse bustled off.

Clara drew a deep breath in relief.

"I am glad I was not cross with her, dear old soul!" was her inward ejaculation. "But it *is* provoking to have *that* interpretation put on the affair, when she always *said*, saucy little thing, that she would not have him!"

And, shaking back her heavy tresses (as was her wont when she wished to shake off some unpleasant thought), and settling her snowy robes, Clara sailed down, swan-like, to the drawing-room. In about a quarter of' an hour arrivals might be expected to commence.

The house was already lighted throughout with soft, shaded lamps; the clustering exotics with which every recess was filled caught the gleam on their dark foliage, while the blossoms showed transparent and many-hued, as if the fairies were holding a mimic illumination of their own.

That atmosphere of light and perfume was Clara's element.

The ball passed off much like other balls on similar occasions. There were, as usual, the vibrating tones of the band, the untiring footsteps of the dancers; there was the supper, laid out in the large conservatory, which had been *cooled* and decorated for the occasion, with pendent lamps gleaming between vine-leaves and tendrils; there were the usual healths and speeches. Except, perhaps, the locality of the supper, the affair had little to boast of in the way of originality; but it was more than commonly successful, as was generally the case with anything into which Clara threw her full energies. And this was for her brother—was, in one sense, her farewell expression of affection. She quite forgot herself; or if she remembered her own inward happiness, it only served to give a softening grace to her manner, sometimes too decided to be winning.

And perhaps it is hardly a correct expression to say that the ball passed off like other balls—even *birthday* balls. There was surely more *heart* in it; a deeper undercurrent of

feeling than is usual even on such special
occasions. All knew the real, though unacknowledged, second meaning of the festival;
all felt that it was Clara's farewell to a circle
wherein she had moved from her earliest girlhood. She had been liked by most, admired
by many, loved by some; her presence, her
very aspect, had been bright and inspiriting;
her departure would leave a void in that
limited sphere, such as can scarcely be con-
ceived by the *habitués* of a wider and more
varied society, where the favourite of one
season vanishes, unmissed and unlamented, to
make room for an equally popular successor.
Among the guests at Mr. Stretton's were few
but would have claimed, by some title or
other, the name of personal *friends;* nearly
all had some real acquaintance with the inner
life of the family, some interest in its individual members, and in any events with which
their weal and woe were bound up. And Clara's
guests, of both sexes and of every age, hung

about her that evening with a spontaneous *empressement* far beyond the observance which the forms of society prescribed; and pressed her hand at parting with a cordial warmth which showed that much which it would have been quite out of rule to express, or even allude to, lay beneath the ordinary routine ceremonial.

CHAPTER IX.

A BRIEF interval succeeded; brief, yet tedious; hurried, yet uncomfortably and unaccountably long. In point of fact, there was barely time for all that had to be accomplished. Among other cogent reasons, or pretexts, for avoiding all unnecessary delay, "the boys" had stood Dr. Harland in good stead. It had been absolutely necessary that they should come home for the ball on brother Edward's birth-day; it was equally necessary that they should grace sister Clara's wedding with their dutiful presence. And their school was too distant for them to return thither in the meantime. And it will easily be understood that a prolongation of their visit, under existing circumstances, was a favour desired by none.

And yet, poor boys! they really were wonderfully good. They were in that state of repressed excitement which can sometimes keep even schoolboys quiet. Their minds were big with the dignity and importance of attending a wedding; with foreshadowings of the eminent position they should occupy, as protectors and masters of the ceremonies to the two little bridesmaids, for whose welldoing, *in all senses*, they were to be solemnly made responsible. They seemed trying, by an instalment of discreet behaviour, to show themselves worthy of so onerous a trust.

Mr. Hurburne, too, behaved wonderfully well; wholly abstaining from annoying Clara, and treating Dr. Harland with marked deference. As for Aunt Sarah, she proved herself, as she had done throughout, to have been well worth waiting for. So things altogether, if not very cheerful just at present, might well have been worse.

Meanwhile the embroidered pocket-hand-kerchief, Mabel's wedding-gift, was nearly completed. Not in all the glory which her imagination had at first portrayed. It was a weakness of Mabel's to dream glorious dreams, and then find herself totally at fault when the dream was to be converted into reality. Here, as in all else, the conception was quick and vivid, the practical power almost wholly wanting. The oak-leaf wreath had to be entirely suppressed, and Mabel's prowess as a needlewoman concentrated exclusively upon the corners. The flying arrow, with its indis-pensable motto, had been pusillanimously left to the last, as the most difficult; but it really was successfully achieved, and Mabel was triumphantly putting in the finishing stitches, when she stopped short, and laid down her work so abruptly that the quiet, plodding German, used as she was to her madcap pupil's vagaries, looked perfectly appalled.

"Mein Gott!—I beg pardon, that you call *swear* in English—but, my child, what is it? what fails thee? Thou hast truly frightened me!"

"I must show this to my aunt directly— before I send it—she will not like it!"

"She *will* like it, you would say," was the governess's matter-of-fact suggestion.

"She will *not* like it! That was what I said, and what I meant," replied Mabel, rather crossly.

"Forgive me, my child! You said—I must show it to her, because she will not like it! What shall that mean?"

"I always mean what I say. My aunt will not like it."

"What a pity! If you had only said so before, some other device might easily have been found!—But the Fräulein thinks not always so much what her aunt likes!"

"No, that is true!" and Mabel could scarcely help laughing. "But when I do what she does not like, I must *tell* her of it."

The good Fräulein still looked puzzled; but the discussion was cut short by Mrs. Stretton herself entering the library, where the governess and pupil were sitting. As usual, she took no notice of what was going on, but was proceeding to look for whatever it was that she herself wanted; but Mabel got up, and intercepted her movements, standing before her with the work in her hand.

"Aunt, this is my wedding present to Clara. I want you to look at it."

Mrs. Stretton took the delicate cambric from her niece, and examined it with that sort of courteous attention which she was ever ready to bestow, even when not in the least interested.

"Ah, very pretty! very proper, my dear!" Suddenly her countenance changed. "You have given her the Stretton crest, I see. Not quite correct, my dear Mabel, for a bride elect. But just as you please."

"I thought you might not like it, aunt."

"My dear Mabel, what can it matter to me? They are Strettons, of course; and the people at the Heralds' Office very properly assign to them the Stretton crest. A crest, you know, is quite arbitrary and unimportant; it is only the armorial bearings which determine the family."

"And they have those nearly the same," Mabel was rashly persisting. But her aunt was evidently determined not to hear or understand.

"A very pretty handkerchief, indeed, Mabel," she said, cutting abruptly across what Mabel was beginning. "Your friend cannot fail to be pleased with it." And with her air of *grande dame* she quitted the room.

Mabel sat for a minute in silence, looking after her rather dolefully. The governess appeared bewildered.

" Ah, well !" and Mabel drew a long breath.
" It can't be helped. I could not send the
handkerchief without showing it to her. Now
I shall make haste and get it finished; and
dear Clara will like it, I know."

And the dainty work was at last brought to
a prosperous termination : was duly admired
and rejoiced over by governess and pupil;—it
did not seem necessary to exhibit it a second
time to Mrs. Stretton ;—was then, by the joint
efforts of Fräulein C. and Mabel, daintily enve-
loped in tissue paper, and swathed in cotton
wool, to prevent rubbing in the long journey
it had to perform. A covering of paper somewhat coarser, but still soft in texture, succeeded ; lastly, the whole was firmly folded in
stout brown paper, carefully secured with
tiny lady-like seals, and directed in Mabel's
best hand,—not so good as might be wished,
and certainly showing to disadvantage upon
the brown paper, which made the up-strokes
especially a labour and sorrow. Luckily a

more favourable specimen was enclosed, in the shape of a delicate triangular billet, carefully ensconced between the wrappings of the parcel. Postage was a consideration in those days. Just as Mabel was painfully endeavouring to repair a faulty letter in the direction, where the pen had stuck obstinately by the way, and left the character incomplete, old Thomas came in upon some slight errand to the young mistress. He never lost an opportunity of hovering about her.

" Oh, Thomas," said Mabel, without raising her eyes from her occupation, " you are just come at the right time. Will you—my aunt will let you, I know—just give this parcel to Clarke the next time you go into the village, and ask him to take great care of it to N., and to see that it goes by the coach ?"

" Yes, miss—yes, surely ;" yet the old man still lingered.

" What is the matter, Thomas ?—To morrow

will do very well, you know, if you are not
going into Ringwood to-day."

"Oh, it is not that, miss ; but—I'll ask
the mistress ; most like she'd have no objection."

"Objection ?—Oh, if that is what you are
afraid of, I can speak to my aunt myself this
minute."

"I did clean the windows thoroughly yesterday, and the furniture was well rubbed
only the other day, and the plate—I think the
mistress would surely not miss (want) me."

"Want you ?—Why should she want you
more than any other time when you go into
the village ?"

"It's not the village I'm thinking on, miss.
But I could get to N—— and back ;—Clarke
would give me a lift ;—let me see—how long
would it take ?"

"You did not understand me, Thomas ; I
only asked you to give Clarke the parcel, that
he may take it over to meet the coach."

" I know what you meaned, miss, very well,"
and Thomas drew himself up, as if a little slur
had been cast upon his sagacity. " But it
goes against me that Clarke should meddle
with this here parcel. His hands are oft-
times none too clean,—saving your presence,
miss; and he carries a sight of queer things
in his cart; and the work that I've seen you
at, early and late, worritin' yourself no end,
and so proud and pleased over it,—I can't
abear that the feller should touch it—God
forgive me for speaking ill of a fellow-creature,
that's made the same as myself. Flesh and
blood shouldn't be a settin' of itself up; I
might have been no better than a common
carrier myself, if it had been His will."

The old man was evidently determined ; so
Mabel compromised the matter, by begging
that he would leave it to her to speak to her
aunt about it. This she did with a considerable feeling of shame and awkwardness at
what appeared so ridiculous a notion as that

Thomas should be sent over express to N——
with her little parcel; the more so, as the
affair of the pocket-handkerchief itself was one
in which Mrs. Stretton evidently found it
difficult to take any interest. But her aunt
cut short her blushing explanations as to old
Thomas having taken this fancy into his head,
with a good-humoured—

"Quite right, my dear; I am glad that
Thomas has so much of the *preux chevalier*
about him. I would be the last to discourage
him in his loyal devotion to his little lady; he
shall go over to N—— by all means,—to-
morrow, if you like. I suppose that will be
soon enough?"

Mrs. Stretton, with all her "stiffness," as
it was usually called, was good-natured. Her
mind was not narrow enough to harass her
household with difficulties and petty inter-
ference about trifles.

So the packet was conveyed in all honour
to N——, and entrusted, with elaborate in-

junctions, to the care of the guard. A simple-looking little packet it was; and in these days would probably have been weighed, stamped, and despatched to the post-office without any such flattering anxiety as to its journey. However, the pains bestowed upon it were not thrown away; without accident, without so much as a soil, it reached London; then, by carrier at last, was forwarded to its destination, and received with full as much surprise and pleasure as had been anticipated.

CHAPTER X.

CLARA was in the library, assisting Aunt Sarah in the despatch of the many little notes which the existing state of affairs rendered necessary.

"How strange it seems," she had just been remarking, "to have no relations to invite! One has friends innumerable ; but there is an odd vacancy in the want of kindred."

Just then the parcel was brought in.

"Little Mab's writing !" was Clara's first exclamation. "The little darling has been devising some present or other, to show that

she does not forget me. Ah! how pretty!"
as the delicate fabric became visible amid its
numerous enfoldings. "I never supposed
that she could work so nicely. And see,
Aunt Sarah!" and Clara held up the corner,
on which her quick glance had espied the
Stretton arrow. "See! that is a token that
she still longs, as she used to do, to claim us
as cousins! The poor little thing always had
a forlorn feeling, when she thought there were
only Arthur and herself; no others, I mean,
of the same blood. Just as I used to do at
school, when I heard all the others talking of
their relations; though *we* were enough in
ourselves. I suppose it was some instinct of
the sort which made me take to Mabel. Did
you ever feel in that way, Aunt Sarah?—as if
you wished to have more people really belonging to you?"

"I don't know, my dear. I had a sister,
you know, poor Ann!—and we were brought
up very quietly, she and I, and your father.

We girls never went to school, or anywhere
from home; so we knew and heard very little
of how things were in other families. And
your grandpapa was very different from your
father; *that, you* can remember, my dear
Clara! A good, kind father he was, but not
indulgent; and would allow no *fancies*, as he
called them. I sometimes think he knew
more than he would say; that my grandfather
might have told him something of who we
were, and where we came from. But he was
always angry at a hint on the subject; if he
knew any thing, no mortal ever would have
induced him to breathe a word regarding it.
Perhaps, if he had not kept all quite so close,
it might have made some difference to *me ;"*
and the transparent cheek grew pink as that of
a girl in her teens. "But all is for the
best; I have had a very happy life; few
are so happy. Only I felt it was but fair to
put Edward in the way of clearing things up,
if I could. Something made me fancy it

might perhaps some day make a difference to *him*."

And the soft hazel eyes fixed themselves on Clara's with an anxious, enquiring glance.

But Clara shrank from the subject. To avoid the gentle gaze, which seemed to ask a confidence she was determined not to give, she began carefully folding up the handkerchief, which she had all this time retained in her hands. As she was smoothing the tissue paper in which it had been wrapped, Mabel's little three-cornered note fell out. It was a welcome diversion; and Clara, opening and glancing through it hastily, read it aloud :

" You know, dear Clara, I cannot work as you do; but I have tried my best, that you might have something really of my own doing. And oh! dear Clara, when the day comes, it will be almost the same as if I were with you; I shall feel so as if I were there; and it almost seems to me as if I should see and hear you all. And you, when you have time to think of anything, I know you will not forget   YOUR LITTLE MABEL.

"My aunt desires me to send her compliments and congratulations."

The postscript was added in a much stiffer hand than the note itself; it had evidently been written with a newly-mended pen; and in all probability had been appended at the last, after the note had been folded up as finished.

"It shall be my wedding handkerchief," said Clara, as she laid the handkerchief and note together carefully aside.

Clara had many wedding-gifts—gifts of intrinsic value, and gifts rendered precious by the feeling they expressed—many which combined both species of worth. Yet she liked Mabel's present one of the best among them, —almost as well, in its way, as the splendid piano which her father gave her; as Aunt

Sarah's exquisite lace, fit for a fairy bridal ; as the pearls which her brother clasped upon her arm ; as the gorgeous tea-caddy, the boys' joint present—(they always connected sister Clara with tea-making);—certainly better than the costly diamond earrings presented to his niece by Mr. Hurburne, a few days before her marriage. Yet Clara was a true woman, and diamonds *were* diamonds in her eyes.

" Papa does not think them quite suitable for me," she said, in a half-deprecating tone to Dr. Harland, as she was somewhat shyly trying on the dazzling ornaments before the drawing-room mirror.

" I don't know," said Dr. Harland ; " you look very well in them, Clara."

So the earrings were forthwith taken into favour, and were worn for the first time on the wedding morning—worn, though not seen : Clara, to Barlow's infinite distress, having insisted that her hair should be so dressed as to hide them. But she did not forget to

lift for one moment the heavy tresses, with a
saucy smile at her uncle when she passed
him in the hall. He and she were uncon-
genial spirits, and something very like a feud
had long smouldered between them; but she
was very happy, and happiness thaws all
animosities in hearts genial enough really to
warm in its sunshine.

It was a gorgeous October day, splendid as
summer, yet with a crisp freshness of aspect
and feeling; a day well befitting the bright-
eyed bride who bore herself so stately amid
the clouds of overshadowing lace; her native
vivacity of look and gesture just softened, but
not subdued. Four-season roses were then
unknown; but the delicate pink monthly
blossoms, mingling with the rarer flowers
which decorated the rooms, diffused a faint
sweetness, harmonizing well with the regretful
joy in every heart. Clara was no angel of
gentleness and perfection; and she was going
to marry happily, to live within easy reach;

but she would be no longer a portion of the daily life in the happy home; and it was like the sudden gloom after sunset when her warm and genial presence was withdrawn.

And all that morning Mabel sat in her recessed bedroom-window, leaning yearningly forward to the far south-east, as if her longing had power to bear her bodily to the scene which her mental eye beheld. Fixed and motionless she sat, as in a trance; then, with one panting exclamation, " Dear, dear Clara !" she sank down before the low window-cushion, and buried her face in her hands, in a child-like paroxysm of sobs and tears.

It was soon over, and she went down-stairs, just the same as usual, except for the entire absence of the wonted colour in her cheeks. Even the placid governess made a sudden exclamation at her pallid aspect; her bloom was so completely a part of herself that the loss of it made her appear a different person. Mrs. Stretton almost started as she first beheld her; but, with her habitual self-possession, she made no observation or enquiry; and, with a quiet but decisive gesture, forbade any further demonstration on the part of the Fräulein. Mabel was accordingly left un-harassed and unmolested, and after a night of heavy, overpowering sleep, she came down to breakfast next morning with eyes and cheeks restored to all their accustomed bright-ness.

CHAPTER XI.

CLARA had of course written at once, in her own warm-hearted style, to thank the little girl for the wedding-gift, on which she plainly saw so much pains and thought had been bestowed. After this, the correspondence rather languished. Mabel, in fact, felt a little shyness of Clara, since the latter had been metamorphosed into that formidable personage, a " married lady."

Since Mabel's residence at Ringwood, it had been almost entirely through Clara that she had received tidings of her grandfather

and grandmother. She had herself written
to them pretty regularly; more so, in fact,
than might have been expected from her age
and desultory habits. But old Mr. and Mrs.
Arleigh, as has been seen, were no great
letter-writers; and their repugnance to the
task naturally increased with every added year
of life. Thus they scarcely ever answered
Mabel's communications, except in the form
of long, involved messages, sent through Miss
Stretton; who, with her characteristic good-
nature, kept up the habit of every now
and then paying them a visit. So that
Mabel now began to feel a double blank in
the suspension of Clara's letters; and yet
she could not make up her mind to ask
her friend to take further trouble on her
account.

Mrs. Stretton, though she made no remark,
perhaps saw, in some degree, the state of the
case; for she had always been accustomed, on
the arrival of a letter from Clara, to enquire,

with her unfailing courtesy, if it contained news of Mr. and Mrs. Arleigh.

" Mabel," she said abruptly one morning, " I do not like that there should be so little communication between you children and your—nearest—relatives. It is not right to Mr. and Mrs. Arleigh. Arthur's school is not so very far from London; I shall make arrangements for him to pay them a visit on his way home for the holidays."

And she left the room, without waiting for an answer ; as was her wont after announcing any determination which either cost her personally some effort, or which, for some other reason, she did not wish discussed.

Edward had, at the moment, unhesitatingly acceded to his father's proposal of enlisting Mabel in the Holmfirth quest ; and several times, in the period of blank dulness which followed Clara's departure, he thought of writing, as Mr. Stretton had suggested, to tell her of the fresh clue they had obtained. But

the letter was never written ; some indefinable
mixture of feelings seemed to induce him day
by day to postpone it. Among these feelings
the preponderating one, perhaps, was his
proud shyness of obtruding on the Ringwood
Strettons an unwelcome kinship.

So Mabel did not appear destined by the
fates to achieve the honours of discovery. It
mattered the less to her at the moment, as she
had just then full occupation for her time and
thoughts. Catherine came back from her
excursion, radiant with health and happiness ;
and held Mabel entranced for hours with her
descriptions of mountain and lake, castle and
cathedral. Thus the autumn wore rapidly on ;
the weird old hawthorns in the Chace were
transmuted into coral bowers, before the notion seemed fairly entertained that winter was
at hand. And then, when the snow began to
lie heavy on the dark plumes of the cedars,
Arthur returned for the holidays ; so ruddy
and joyous that a new life seemed infused

into the grey old house, and its stately, care-worn mistress.

Arthur had a little dreaded the visit to grandpapa and grandmamma; but all had passed off well. Grandpapa had not been at all cross, and had given him some apples to eat on the journey; and grandmamma had hardly cried at all when he came away, and had said how pleased she was to see him so well and happy.

Even Frank came home for a brief Christmas respite; and Catherine, on whom her constitutional languor was just beginning again to steal, roused up at once in the delight of his presence. A new and happier under-standing seemed, in their brief *téte-à-téte* jour-ney, to have sprung up between the brother and sister.

Happy in her renewed certainty of her brother's affection, and bent upon pleasing him, Catherine shook off more and more of her dreamy apathy; gliding almost imperceptibly,

with her own timid grace, into the position
which he wished her to assume, as the young
head of the establishment.

The preceding Christmas (the first after
the death of the young heir of the Chace)
had indeed been celebrated in Mrs. Stretton's
household with every due observance: punc-
tiliously so, perhaps; for all feared, by the
omission of any outward sign of rejoicing, to
remind themselves or others of the underlying
grief. Now, however, the memory of that
loss was deadened in all hearts, except, perhaps, that of the childless mother; and even
she could scarcely feel herself longer childless,
so strongly had her love and pride entwined
themselves around this second Arthur, the representative of her lost son. She never in
words designated him as her heir; but all
understood the gesture, half proud, half caress-
ing, with which she leaned on his shoulder as
she led him down the long files of tables, where
servants and retainers were marshalled to

their Christmas cheer; and then, returning
to the upper end, while all still remained
standing, bade them—

"Drink *Master Arthur's* health!" But
none guessed by what an effort that clear
voice was steadied for the command.

Arthur himself thought and cared nothing
about the heirship; but those were merry holidays to him. He was always happy near
his aunt; and Mabel was not yet grown too
womanly to share in most of his pastimes, or
to enter with zest into his details of school
frolics; she was used to schoolboys; John and
Fred had pretty well accustomed her to the
peculiar ways and notions of the class. But
in addition to this home companionship, Arthur and Frank had struck up a fast friend-
ship. Notwithstanding the difference of age,
the two seemed to take to each other. Mrs.
Stretton would trust Arthur anywhere with
Frank; so Frank took the boy to skate on the
wide river; or accompanied him in long

scrambling expeditions over the slippery, frosted downs, when Mabel was rigorously confined to the terraces and garden walks. And, in return, Arthur shut himself up for hours to work upon his unfinished likeness of Catherine, which he persisted in allowing no member of the Chace family to behold; but when he had tolerably satisfied himself with his performance, he gave it to Frank, with strict injunctions to hang it up in his London chambers, where it might put him in mind of Catherine when he was away from her.

"Well, Cathie," said her brother, a day or two before leaving, "I shall soon run down again to have a glimpse of you; meanwhile, remember that you are mistress here. You are beginning to enjoy presiding over your home, are you not, Catherine?"

The last words broke involuntarily from his lips. Catherine's eyes had before been cast down, to hide the tears that filled them; now she raised them quickly, with a half-puzzled, half deprecating expression; but turning the matter off lightly, she only replied—

"Is it not rather hard-hearted of you, Frank, to wish me to set my affections on a dignity which some new sister may any day force me to abdicate?"

Frank started as if he had been stung.

"Catherine, let me never hear anything of this sort from you again! I beg your pardon, dear! Have I frightened you?" And kissing her, he left the room.

It was a pity that one harsh word—harsher than he had ever addressed to her—should mar the happiness of those else unclouded days; but he managed, in the brief remaining period of his stay, wholly to charm away Catherine's returning timidity, and left her laughing and colouring at his parting information, that he carried her portrait with him, carefully packed in his portmanteau. She had herself never heard of it since she had sat to Arthur for the likeness.

But Arthur had now more ambitious projects in his head.   Among the stock-books at
his school was an old "Poetical Primer," well
thumbed and dog's-eared by successive gene-
rations of pupils, broken-backed, and deficient
as to title-page.   In this book he had met
with Collins' "Ode on the Passions," that
splendid, unique poem, which can never grow
old or obsolete, let allegory go out of date as
it may.   And Arthur had just then a true
boyish passion for allegory ; he revelled, as so
many have done, and will do, in the profuse
and vivid imagery of this poem, and was now
bent on a grand picture, in which Mabel was
to present Hope, and Catherine, Melancholy.
Now the casting of parts was by no means
unexceptionable ; but there was no´ choice.
Mabel's shadowy grey eyes were very unlike
the " eyes so fair " of the poem ; the hair had
not precisely the "golden" hue required.   But
hair could easily be altered in a painting ;
even eyes, on an emergency.   These were

minor points. But it was no small strain on his conversational powers to make Mabel *smile* just when he required it. Her smiles always came and went, in a way that might have baffled a more experienced artist, and were replaced by a variety of graver expressions, all more or less inappropriate to the present subject. Catherine, however, was still more provoking; she would not look half as *melancholy* as was required.

"I cannot think what has come to you both," he at last impatiently exclaimed. "When I first read the poem, Catherine, I thought directly what a capital 'Melancholy' you would make; and now,—I suppose, it's being so much with Mabel, for you have quite caught some of her looks. And Mabel herself, she has grown graver, I think."

As was to be expected under such˙discouraging circumstances, the picture made but slow progress, and was left, with many another vision, to be realized "next holidays."

For these pleasant Christmas holidays, like other pleasant things, came all too soon to an end. And Mabel missed Arthur the more, because Catherine, less hardy than herself, could not face wind and weather, as she, bred in a Welsh cottage, had done from infancy, without injury. So on many a bleak, rough day of early spring, she had to take her rambles alone.

But the dull days passed quickly away; the wild white wind-flowers quivered in countless profusion in the sunny glades of the Chace; and Catherine, though no great walker, could again mount her beautiful Zorah, and accompany Mabel in whatever direction the variable whims of the latter might impel her. After a ride together, Mabel generally escorted her companion to Calder House, then rode home alone, cantering saucily across the turf, to peep in at the windows of Mrs. Stretton's business room, before dismounting at the hall-door. Catherine would have been too timid to ride back alone.

One day, just as she was thus returning home, she was met on the steps by her aunt.

"My dear Mabel," began Mrs. Stretton, abruptly, "you really are growing so tall, it looks quite ridiculous to see you on that pony."

Mabel laughed.

"Why, Catherine is taller than I am."

"Yes, but her pony is quite different from yours. Puck did very well while you were quite a child ; but——"

"Am I not a child now?" asked Mabel, drawing up her head a little, laughing and blushing at the same time.

"You are certainly old enough to be wiser," said Mrs. Stretton, laughing in her turn; "but I cannot have you look ridiculous in the neighbourhood. I must inquire about a horse for you at once." ·

Fain would Mabel have remonstrated. Puck

was all she wished, and they were old friends; besides, she could not bear that her aunt, who denied herself every luxury, should go to this additional expense for her. But no one ever remonstrated with Mrs. Stretton; it was too evidently useless.

CHAPTER XII.

THE London season began; and young Mrs. Harland's diamond earrings, no longer hidden, flashed through many a gay party, where the pretty young wife of the distinguished physician was an object of very ge neral attention. And Clara's saucy eyes, and curving throat, bespoke anything but dissatisfaction with her position.

And, in truth, she was as happy as possible. She had given up her whole heart to her husband, with a complete devotion, which contrasted curiously with the struggle it had cost her, and with her former impatience of any influence that threatened to trench upon her independence of thought and action.

Nor was affection the only bond; there was a curious congeniality of taste and feeling.

Both delighted in society—in the exercise of a hospitality which was only not ostentatious, because so spontaneous and unconscious; in all the details even of social life and duty; in having things go off well; in the skilful combination into a harmonious whole of the most seemingly heterogeneous elements. One of these social successes, achieved where the timid or the awkward would have failed, was a triumph for both; and in both the goodnatured pleasure in seeing people pleased with each other very much predominated over any personal pride in the tact by which the amalgamation had been achieved.

Dr. Harland, after a severe preliminary struggle, had been eminetly successful in his profession; he now worked as hard in it for love as he had formerly done for a living. But his buoyant, joyous nature required and enjoyed the relief of other pursuits, after the tension to which it was subjected for many hours of the day. His keen, critical zest for art was both companionship and culture to Clara's untrained enthusiasm; and he was gradually beguiling his young wife into something very like his own passionate enjoyment of music. He felt at ease in indulging these tastes; for their mother's rather large fortune was settled on his children; his own position, and Clara's portion, left him no scruples about pleasing her and himself in these matters, or humouring her in a few little congenial pomps and vanities, which he could sympathize with, if not share; whereas her father, so indulgent in all else, had ever checked, with almost puritanic sternness, aught that could be construed as tending towards display. And even he, now that he was no longer responsible for

her proceedings, only laughed, and good-
humouredly enjoyed *her* enjoyment.

She was beginning to fancy that the London Square, still stately, though fallen from its
first fashion, had its own characteristic charm;
to find a certain sombre grandeur in the great
well-staircase, the lofty, resounding house,—
the Turkey-carpeted dining-room, and crimson-
damasked drawing-rooms, of her new home.
A lighter grace was easily given, and could
not long be absent, where Clara presided.

But the children?

They certainly were a great vexation to her!
They were so pale and thin, it made her
miserable to look at them; she was positively
ashamed for any stranger to see them; their
looks would all be set down to unkindness or
neglect on the part of the stepmother. So
she was never easy when they were out of her
sight; took them with her, walking or driv-
ing, wherever she went; seemed to have well-
nigh ceased to care for her favourite picture-

galleries, so absorbing was her interest in zoological gardens, feats of horsemanship, or whatever else lighted up those little pale faces with childish bloom and brightness.

"You don't know how Edward scolded me before I was married; he fancied that I accepted you because——When I was a silly girl, I used to say I would never marry a man in business."

"Did you?" said Dr. Harland, quietly. "I was very near being one myself."

"You were?" said Clara, eagerly.

"It seems that in that case I should not have had my pretty little wife."

Clara gave him a saucy look, but seemed to consider any reply unnecessary.

"But my father was ruined, duped by a swindler; and a terrible disappointment it was to me, to be sent to learn medicine of a distant relation, a country surgeon, who took me to educate out of kindness."

"You never told me all this," said Clara, with unusual softness.

"It is a painful subject; and besides, in some cases, one can *forgive* only by *forgetting*."

"But you like your profession now?" said Edward.

"Why, if one has to do a thing at all, one likes to do it decently, and then one gets fond of the thing itself; and one is glad to help poor creatures when one can. But it is wretched, uncertain work," said Dr. Harland, throwing himself wearily back in his chair. "One longs for the certainty there is in some sciences — so much power applied, such and such proportionate results — instead of groping in the dark, fighting with an enemy whose strength one cannot measure."

Here occurred one of the "interruptions" which Clara had so much disliked the thought of; some one was suddenly and alarmingly ill, and Dr. Harland was implored to come without delay.

In a moment he had started up from his luxurious chair, and was down in the hall, laughing at Clara, who had followed, entreating him to be careful about the cold. It was a bleak spring night.

She came back slowly to the drawing-room, and returned shivering to the fireside.

"After all, Edward," said his sister, settling herself again in her lounging chair by the fire, which glistened cheerily on her silk dress and bright face, "you had not much right to quarrel with me on the score of pride. How does your interest about our descent from the Ringwood Strettons agree with your allegiance to your 'patrimony,' as you call our grandfather's business?"

"If one person can combine the two feelings, it proves that they are not incompatible," replied Edward, somewhat oracularly.

"Your 'little wife,' however, will soon learn

at Ringwood to view such things diffe-
rently."

Clara repented this speech the moment she
saw how painfully Edward coloured.

"You do not mean," she exclaimed, "that
you really——"

"Nonsense, Clara! she was but a child,"
said Edward, impatiently. "But I must be
off," he added, hastily, rising and looking at
his watch; "I said I should be home early.
Good-bye, Clara; bid Harland goodnight for
me." And he was off before she had time to
remonstrate.

And the Ringwood descent ceased, from
that day, to be a favourite topic for half-
playful, half-earnest chat between the brother
and sister. To Clara, absorbed in her new
interests, engrossed by new affections, wholly
satisfied with her new happiness, it seemed
already but a reminiscence of childish folly,
retaining not even enough of reality to make
it amusing as a passing jest.

But Clara was beginning to reproach herself with having neglected — for the time almost forgotten—her little Mabel. Her conversation with Edward, bringing the child's image vividly before her, supplied just the needed stimulus to her good intentions of writing. The result was a long, affectionate letter ; really *long*, even from Clara,—full of her own happiness, but full also of her old warm interest in all that concerned Mabel. It brought a speedy answer ; and as that morning Dr. Harland, having no pressing engagement, seemed disposed to lounge over his breakfast, Clara, in the intervals of coffee-pouring, read aloud the letter, in which, as in all of Mabel's, the name of " Catherine " frequently recurred.

" I am glad," observed Dr. Harland, " that the poor child has such a pleasant companion ; but what is this ' Catherine's ' other name ?"

" Calder," replied Clara. " Calder House is close to the Chace, I fancy."

"How strange," exclaimed Dr. Harland, "that I should not have heard of it before!"

"How should you?" said Clara, surprised; "I scarcely know of her but as Catherine. Do you know the Calders?"

"They were far-away connections of poor Mary's (his first wife). I never understood exactly how; one of those round-about kinships which may be anything or nothing, according as the parties happen to suit. My wife was very fond of the old lady, the grandmother; so they made the most of the cousinship—I forget how many degrees removed, or on which side it came. Since then the thing has dropped; this young fellow is odd and reserved; I can't make him out. I have asked him to come here, however, till I am tired, and have given it up as hopeless. Perhaps you would like to see him, and talk to him about Mabel?" he added, in an altered tone, as the idea occurred to him for the first time. " I'll make one more attempt, if you would."

"Oh! thank you!" said Clara. " But I suppose he won't come?"

" Not very likely! we can but try."

The chance appeared so slight, that Clara did not dwell upon it; and the subject had almost passed from her mind; when, some days after, her husband quite startled her by the energy with which he exclaimed, on entering—

" Clara! he positively *will* come!"

" Who?" asked Clara, bewildered.

" Why, young Calder, whom we were speaking of the other day. I ran against him this morning, and invited him; when, to my amazement, he accepted! I suppose he must have heard of my pretty little wife, and be curious to see her."

Clara laughed and coloured. " I don't like people who make their company such a favour!" she said, rather petulantly.

"Oh! he's not that sort of fellow at all! only odd."

"When will he come?"

"To-morrow. So write a note as quickly as you can to your father and Edward; I hope they will be able to come; they will like to hear about the child."

Frank came at the appointed time; and Clara wondered what her husband had meant by calling him strange and reserved. He evidently felt her no stranger, but was prepared beforehand to like, almost to trust her. They were soon talking together, more like old friends than new acquaintances.

She for some time controlled her own desire to ask about Mabel, from a feeling of delicacy, fearing that Mr. Calder might think it a bad compliment if he imagined *that* the motive of the invitation. At last, as the subject did not seem to arise naturally, she plunged into it with point-blank enquiries as to Mabel's health, happiness, and general position.

But now her contentment with her guest greatly diminished; and the words, "odd and reserved," instead of being inapplicable, seemed coined for the very purpose of describing his manner.

—Yes, she was a very nice little girl;—he was very glad his sister had such a companion. —Oh! yes, she was very happy, he believed; she was generally extremely merry; and seemed indulged in every respect. But he saw very little of her; he was so little at home.—

In this style the conversation was awhile laboriously dragged on; but it was evident nothing worth hearing was to be elicited. Clara, quite provoked, abruptly changed the subject, and alluded to it no more, till after their guest's departure; when she relieved herself by expressing her indignation in the little family conclave.

"He evidently does not in the least appreciate Mabel; he speaks of her just as of any ordinary child. I do not believe he has ever particularly noticed her in any way."

"He seems a good sort of fellow, though," said Edward. "I asked him to dine with us on Tuesday, sir (turning to his father); but he said he would rather come when we were quite alone. I had told him we had two or three friends coming to us that day."

"You must not be annoyed, Edward, at his slipping out of your invitations," said Dr. Harland. He generally serves everybody the same; only with you he has had the grace to make something like an excuse; whereas he tells *me* point-blank that he would rather not come."

"But he *is* coming," said Edward. "He asked if Thursday would suit us; so it is fixed for that day. I don't know whether we dare ask *you*, Clara; will it come within the bond? Do you count for *company* yet at home?"

From that day, imperceptibly to themselves, and rather to the perplexity of bystanders, the

acquaintance between Edward Stretton and
Frank Calder became more and more inti-
mate; ripening by degrees into a fast friend-
ship, closer and more entirely congenial than
either of them had before known. Frank's
reserve, which kept most people aloof, was the
very opposite of his real nature, and was, in
fact, only the result of circumstances, by which
a character, originally open and joyous, had
been, as it were, overlaid, but never wholly
effaced ; while Edward's cheerful ease of manner really served to veil that intense fasti-
diousness of temperament which made him
well nigh impenetrable to many who considered themselves his intimates. In neither
was the reserve *intentional;* and, singularly
enough, neither ever even perceived it in the
other. The two opposite temperaments, by
some happy chance, harmonized without an
effort; in the intercourse between them, neither
was ever conscious of a jarring contact.

CHAPTER XIII.

MRS. STRETTON, not perhaps very wisely, had left the choice of Mabel's new horse pretty much to herself. That is, among several which were pronounced, on competent authority, to be sound and free from vice, she was allowed the selection. And Mabel, of course, chose the most " spirited."

Now " spirited" is not a very alarming word when used of a rough little Shetland pony; but it is something rather different when applied to a fiery chestnut mare. However, saucy as Gypsey might be, it appeared evident that Mabel was quite able to manage her. But Mrs. Stretton very naturally insisted that with such a horse there must be no riding without an attendant; and even announced her immediate intention of adding a trustworthy groom to her establishment.

To the two girls this notion was insupportable. A cabinet council was forthwith holden between them on the occasion.

"Suppose," said Catherine, catching at a forlorn hope, "suppose we ask Frank to ride with us? He will be at home now for a long while, I daresay; he said he should not go anywhere this vacation. That will be better than having a servant after us, at any rate; and when he goes back to London your aunt may be used to the horse, and not mind—or we may think of some other plan."

Mabel considered the matter a few minutes.

"Don't you think it a good plan?" asked Catherine, rather disappointed.

"Yes,—I daresay it is," said Mabel, doubtfully, "if he will not mind the trouble."

Catherine indignantly repudiated the idea of Frank's "*minding.*" "You know he always does anything I wish," she urged, with very unflattering frankness.

It was agreed that the affair should be left in her hands; and under her able negociation all was soon arranged, and the difficulty staved off, for the present at least.

Even with this great improvement on what they had anticipated, both the girls felt at first some regret at the loss of their former wild independence; by degrees, however, as the counterbalancing advantages of an escort developed themselves, they grew more than reconciled. Under Frank's protection they were allowed an unlimited range, instead of being confined, as heretofore, to the precincts of the Chace. As a guide too, their companion was invaluable; familiar as he was from his own school-days with every nook of

the wild country around, well able to pilot
them along tangled wood-paths, where the
dusky-green twilight overhead rendered a
perfect strain of caution necessary, so thickly
were the tree-roots muffled in moss and fern;
—up difficult hill-sides, or along sunken roads,
slippery with protruding ledges of rock.

As a boy, Frank had almost lived on horseback; and at college had rather enjoyed exci-
ting the wonder of his compeers at his daring
feats. Therefore the horse which he hired (for
even Catherine could not persuade him to buy
one) was not likely to be a very tame, unambi-
tious animal. Indeed, he and Mabel had often
some difficulty in curbing their own and their
horses' longing for a wild scour over the open
downs, stretching so temptingly all around,
with no boundary but the deep blue sky.
But Catherine was neither very strong nor
very courageous, and her companions, for her
sake, kept their horses well in hand; while her
gentle Arab, which could probably have out-

stripped both the others, conformed without a sign of impatience to the moderate pace which suited her best. And Catherine, the yielding, unselfish Catherine, was never allowed to suspect that a sacrifice was made for her; or her enjoyment in her rides would have been at an end.

And merry rides they were, after all. Even Frank, on horseback, became his natural joyous self.

One morning, however, Catherine begged off. She had been standing in the sun, cutting the withered blossoms from her rose-trees, till she was tired and dizzy, and fit only to lie down in some cool room. Her companions both protested against going without her; but she declared that in that case she certainly *would* accompany them, at the risk of falling off her horse, or making herself ill. So there seemed no help for it; and after seeing her settled on her sofa, under Mrs. Elliott's care, they set forth.

By a tacit consent Frank and Mabel at once involuntarily guided their horses in the direction which both liked best ; towards the wide, open downs, whence Mabel could catch a glimpse, on clear days, of her beloved sea. The moment she felt the free air of the uplands, she suddenly broke short in their former desultory chat, and exclaiming—" Now let us go fast !" put her horse to its utmost speed. When they reached the famous " seaview" point, the horses were snorting and panting, the riders breathless, and quite disposed for a pause.

But no sea-view was there ; the air was hot and breezeless, laden with heavy vapour from the lower level which they looked down upon ; lurid cloud-shadows lay like blots on the fair, wide landscape. Yet the two riders looked down long, more fascinated than by the usual summer beauty.

" Mabel !" said Frank, suddenly, " I want to ask you something."

"What?" inquired Mabel, surprised.

"Suppose any one you care for had done something very, very wrong?"

"Everybody does, I suppose, sometimes," said Mabel; "I am sure *I* often do."

"Ah, Mabel, but I mean something quite different; something worse than you would ever think of."

"But no one I love ever *would* do such a thing; I should never love anybody who could."

"Look, Mabel!" exclaimed Frank, abruptly. "See how the clouds are gathering! and it feels just like a storm! Let us make haste home! Quick! quick!"

And a wild scour home they had; but no storm came on. As they entered the village, both involuntarily drew rein, and looked at each other, as if questioning the cause of this wild haste.

"There has been no storm, after all," observed Mabel.

"And I have frightened you, and hurried you home in this mad way! Are you very tired? You look quite pale."

"Oh, no, not at all; you know I like to go at full speed."

"Then you have been afraid of a storm?"

"No, I cannot have been afraid; I always enjoy thunder and lightning so much."

"Then what is it?—What would you like to do?"

They were now close at Calder House gates.

"Please," said Mabel, very faintly, "let me come in; to Catherine."

Frank started. "Catherine!" he repeated, in a stifled voice. But as he looked at Mabel, he saw that her very lips were turning white. Springing off his horse, he managed to steady her on her saddle with one hand, while with the other he opened one leaf of the gate; then, still steadying her, he drew her horse in, his own following.

But now the light had come back into Mabel's eyes, though the colour had not yet returned to her cheeks. As they stopped at the 'house door, she was off the horse in a minute, without help, in her old childish way.

"Oh, thank you, Mr. Calder! Don't be afraid about me; I am quite well again. I will just run up to see Catherine."

And she had reached the foot of the stairs, when she suddenly turned, and came back for a minute.

"You really are not frightened about me? You were very kind; but you see I am quite well now." And quite well she looked, with her own glowing and changing colour in her cheeks.

With one half-wistful look, as if to assure herself that his alarm was at an end, she was off again.

Yet all that afternoon Mabel was oppressed by a strange sense of dread, for which she could not account; it might be something in the atmosphere. The sunset seemed to throw such a lurid, brassy light on the old purple beech by the library window; she wondered she had never observed it so before. And though at night she had no distinct dreams, she woke with an anxious, harassed feeling, quite unlike herself.

" Let *me* off to-day, Cathie, dear," she petitioned, when Frank and Catherine rode over to fetch her.

" Why, dearest Mabel, are you ill?" said Catherine, quite alarmed.

" Oh, no, not the least."

"Then let us have no such nonsense, Mabel," interposed Mrs. Stretton, sharply. " You are keeping Miss Calder waiting."

Mabel almost cowered beneath her aunt's severity, and came forward silently to be helped on to her horse; Frank saying, in an under tone, as he did so—

" You know, if you do not feel well, we can stop at Calder House."

But when they reached Calder House, she protested she was well,—quite well ;—should enjoy a ride.

—" Only if Catherine would let me ride her horse, just for a change."

It was a mere whim, arising, perhaps, from her restless, uncomfortable mood ; and partly, perhaps, from an unavowed feeling that the high action of her own horse would be too much that day for her strength.

" Oh, to be sure, if you wish it, dear," replied Catherine, at once preparing to dis- mount.

" Can you manage Gypsey, Catherine ?" asked her brother.

" Do you mean to affront me ?" was the laughing rejoinder.

And very well she did manage Gypsey, and many were the glances of pleased surprise cast on her by Frank during that day's ride. And Mabel's spirits rose rapidly, with the luxurious sensation of being borne along, without effort, through the balmy summer air.

On their way home, as they were riding leisurely along a narrow lane leading to the village, a little dog sprang through a gap in the hedge, barking violently. All three horses suddenly swerved aside ; Catherine, losing her presence of mind, pulled Gypsey's curb rein more sharply than the sensitive animal could bear. A short scuffling noise of rearing and prancing alarmed her companions, but to no purpose. Catherine was thrown violently to the ground ; not dangerously hurt, so far as Frank and Mabel could ascertain ; but sufficiently stunned, bruised, and shaken to alarm even those more experienced or less attached.

CHAPTER XIV.

"CLARA," said her husband, one morning at breakfast, "can you stand a scientific dinner-party?"

"I will promise to sit through it, at all events," said Clara, laughing; "and if I open my ears, perhaps I may improve my mind."

"Don't flatter yourself with that hope," said Dr. Harland, "they will be miles too deep for you, and for me too, most likely; though it is my business to know about such things, and I have a fancy for them, too, which I don't think you have, my busy bird."

" I confess, said Clara, " I never had patience to read books on such subjects, though I
like to be told the pretty bits. But who are
these formidable visitors ?"

" Why, Clara, I really ought to invite
Wrotham to dinner. He is a rough bear,
but has been always remarkably civil to me ;
sent me a card for his lectures, when none
could be got for money."

" *Pray* ask him," said Clara ; " I will be
as civil as I can, in return."

" Yes, but we can't have him *alone ;* and
he has no notion of general society ; always
fancies himself in the lecture-room, and goes
on for ever deeper and deeper, till people are
driven wild. I must have one or two men
pretty nearly up to his own mark, to meet
him. I know some that would be glad of
the chance of pumping him, and yet that can
hold their own, and keep him a little in check.
But it would be unbearable for you, Clara,
and for me too. I go to his lectures, but I

don't want '*shop*' at my own house, after a
hard morning's round. So we'll invite some
nice pleasant people besides, to make the
thing cheerful. The knowing ones will be
engrossing company for each other; and I
can catch, with one ear, the drift of what they
are after, and throw in a word now and then.
But how late it is!" looking at his watch.
" Good-bye! I must be off!" And in his
usual rapid manner, he was out of the house
in a minute.

That evening, however, the programme of
the proposed dinner-party was discussed in
detail, and the invitations written. It was a
little combat with difficulties, such as Clara
always enjoyed, her spirits rising with the
exigency.

Next day but one, the morning post coming
in, as usual, at breakfast-time—

" Here's a piece of work!" exclaimed Dr.
Harland, throwing down some notes which
had been brought to him. He rose impa-

tiently from the table, and stood before the fire, though the warmth of the spring morning had rendered it scarcely bearable.

" Why, how you frightened me !" said Clara. " What *is* the matter ?"

" Morris and Belinghey can't come; both engaged."

" How unfortunate ! Must we put off the party ?"

" We *cannot;* for Wrotham has accepted,— and I suppose every one besides," he added, glancing towards the notes which his wife had received.

Clara handed them to him.

" All acceptances, of course ! Was there ever such a fix ?"

Clara looked dismayed.

" I will listen as well as I can."

" That will never do ; he has a curious instinct as to whether people understand him or not."

" I can't promise not to look stupid."

"And I can't have you victimized, or our friends either. He will seize on me, and drag me into some discussion, so that I shall not be able to attend to anyone else ; or he will bore them all to death, unless he has one in particular to fasten on."

Clara did not like being baffled.

"Surely there is some one else we might ask ?"

"Why, the difficulty is this :—an ignoramus won't do; Wrotham would be out of patience. One in his own line won't do, unless somewhat on his own level; Wrotham would browbeat him."

"A pleasant individual !" said Clara, laughing. "I wish I could help you; but our family are sadly deficient in such matters. My uncle, indeed——" she stopped short.

"Mr. Hurburne ? is he up in these things ?"

"I know he has always had a great taste that way; and I have heard people, who I

suppose are good judges, say that his knowledge was really wonderful for a man so diffe-
rently occupied."

" Just what we want ; do write and ask
him, as a great favour, to come and help us.
I wonder I never had any notion before that
he had a turn that way. A wonderful man,
really ! Such a fine taste in pictures, and a
shrewd man of business with it all;—this
last is quite a new light to me. I have not
seen half enough of him ; and I scarcely seem
to have heard anything about your uncle from
you, Clara ; you hardly ever mention him."

" Perhaps," said Clara, colouring, " I have
been afraid I might hardly do him justice.
And I am sure we are very good friends—
only all people are not equally congenial."

" Well, I remember thinking from the first
that there was a little ' attraction of repul-
sion' between you and Mr. Hurburne ; but
you never said anything to me about it."

" He was our mother's brother," said Clara,

softly; "and besides, it was a mere childish antipathy, not worth speaking of. I am ashamed of it now."

"My good Clara!" said her husband, "then pray arrange this matter for me, dear; it will be a real service."

Like many things that are expected to be failures, the dinner-party proved a decided success. There were really some most agreeable people; and the conversation never flagged; none of those pauses, so inexplicable and so awkward, during which every one tries in desperation to find something to say, feeling it all the time an impossibility that anything should occur to him; and which are only broken at last by some self-sacrificing individual flinging himself into the chasm, or, in plain English, perpetrating some remark deficient in grammar, sense, appropriateness, and coherence, which sets the whole party at ease, probably by the assurance it inspires that they *can* say nothing quite as bad.

Edward, who watched proceedings anxiously, for Clara's sake, perceived from the first that Wrotham and Mr. Hurburne would *do* together. The marked deference of Mr. Hurburne's manner, combined as it was with a quick and discriminating appreciation, evidently propitiated the man of science, whose conversation, on the other hand, Mr. Hurburne would have considered a boon well worth travelling miles to attain.

Dr. Harland, for some time, hovered skilfully on the outskirts of their discourse, until perfectly satisfied that all was going well; then, with a relieved mind, he left them to themselves, and gave his undivided attention to his other guests.

Edward had also dismissed the affair from his thoughts, and had well-nigh forgotten the presence of the two gentlemen, as they sat conversing together in undertones at the farther end of the table; when, in a momentary lull of the general cheerful buzz, his ear was caught by the sound of Wrotham's voice, raised in peculiarly emphatic tones, as if impressing upon his hearer a point of some especial importance.

"Yes! that bit of land would make the fortune of any one who could get hold of it, and knew how to work it properly."

"Ah!" said Edward, laughing, "that sounds generally interesting!"—

But he was turning away, carelessly, to join again in the general conversation, when a servant, entering the room, approached his master with an ominous look and whisper.

Dr. Harland started up, with a trepidation very unusual in him. "Excuse me,"—to his guests—then, seeing his wife turn pale— "Don't be frightened, Clara; I will be back in a minute." And he hurriedly left the room.

An uncomfortable hush ensued; broken presently by Mr. Stretton and Edward, who tried, by desultory remarks, in a tone of forced cheerfulness, to reassure Clara, and turn the attention of their guests. But something in Dr. Harland's manner had conveyed the unmistakable impression that this was more than an ordinary professional interruption. Wrotham, however, who seemed to have paused only in surprise at the general silence, at once resumed the thread of his discourse, and was listened to by Mr. Hurburne with his former absorbed attention ; when they were again interrupted by the return of Dr. Harland, muffled up in preparation for a night journey.

" It is Catherine Calder," he explained, hurriedly ; " the poor child has had an accident— a fall from her horse. No bones broken, nor any great harm done, I hope ; but she seems so sinking, they have got frightened, and have sent a post-chaise for me ;—no confidence in the country doctors."

*   *   *   *   *

It was a long, dreary night-journey ; and through all those tedious hours Calder House was sleepless with suspense. The sufferer alone, for whom the whole household was wakeful, seemed gradually to sink into the heavy slumber of exhaustion. Mrs. Stretton, who had established herself in unquestioned authority over the sick-room, drove Mabel thence, with the legalized barbarity of her office; bidding her go to bed quietly, and not disturb Catherine. Mrs. Elliott's housewifely care had indeed provided all needful sleeping accommodation for the two unexpected guests. But nothing was farther from Mabel's thoughts. As Catherine's door was closed upon her, she ran down-stairs like one pursued; passed through the gloomy, half-lighted drawing-room, and took refuge in the "little room"— Catherine's little room—beyond; and there, kneeling before a low chair, her face buried in the cushion, she remained, she knew not how long—in something between an agony of prayer and the stupor of overpowering wretchedness.

She was roused by footsteps in the next room—heavy, impatient footsteps—pacing the long apartment almost fiercely up and down, as if desperately endeavouring to leave some insupportable misery behind. The footsteps could not be mistaken; nor the words—"I cannot bear it! I cannot bear it!"—almost equally fierce and impatient, which broke forth at intervals.

With one quick dart Mabel was in the room.

"Will you not forgive me?"—Her gesture was as if she would have knelt down before him; then, crimsoning all over with instantaneous self-recollection, she passed through the outer door, up the stairs, and into the little bedroom assigned for her use, locking the door behind her.

The morning was grey and chilly when the post-chaise drove up to Calder House. The wide, wooden flaps of the entrance-gates were open, so that the office of the old gardener, who stood by them, was merely nominal. The

old man looked pinched and shrunken, with
an expression upon his weather-beaten face of
patient anxiety that was really touching.   He
bowed humbly as the carriage passed him;
then quietly closed the gates, and betook himself silently to the back entrance; to await, in
some one of the least-frequented offices, the
first report of the doctor's opinion.

The hall-door, like the gates, had been
opened without a summons.   "Dr. Harland,
sir, I presume," suggested the butler, blandly.
He could have no possible doubt on the subject; the enquiry was merely a courteous for-
mula on his part; and receiving in reply an
assenting nod, he ushered Dr. Harland into
the large, dull dining-room, where a repast,
something between supper and breakfast,
awaited his arrival.

Despite his professional *sang-froid*, Dr.
Harland could not sit down without the hurried enquiry—"Miss Calder not worse, I
hope?"

"No, sir; that is, we flatter ourselves, sir, there is no alteration for the worse at present, sir."

Before the deliberately-enunciated reply was half completed, the doctor, who was really nearly famished, had begun his attack on the pigeon-pie.

Mrs. Stretton considerately allowed some time to elapse before she made her appearance.

—Catherine was sleeping, she then said; Hannah would bring word when she wakened.

"It is very kind of you to come so promptly, Dr. Harland," she continued. "I should not myself feel the least alarm about Catherine, except that she is so very delicate, which might make anything more serious in her case. But her brother is half wild about her; and my poor little madcap niece, who thinks it is all her fault—"

Mrs. Stretton's voice positively faltered. But she was her usual self the next moment, and entered quietly into a general conversation, which lasted till Hannah appeared, to usher them to the bedside of the patient.

Poor Catherine looked sadly wan and transparent, and her sweet eyes had a misty languor about them, as if they scarcely took cognizance of external objects. The verdict, however, was favourable. "There was no need for alarm; she only required care."

When the examination was over, and Mrs. Stretton, Mrs. Elliott, Frank, and Dr. Harland, were assembled in the drawing-room, Frank said, quietly, "Mrs. Stretton, will you not send for Miss Arleigh?"

Mabel had not appeared, and no one seemed to miss her. Mrs. Stretton, indeed, supposed her to be in bed; and Frank had stood perfectly silent and motionless by his sister's bedside, until satisfied as to Dr. Harland's opinion.

Mabel had not been in bed; she obeyed the summons instantly—quite white, and unnaturally calm, like a criminal expecting sentence.

"Why, Miss Arleigh," said Dr. Harland, "there is no need to look so frightened; Miss Catherine is not going to die;" and he drew her kindly towards him.

But Mabel, the unnatural tension relaxed, was now sobbing like a child, as she indeed was.

"It was all my fault! and he was—they all were—so unhappy!"

"Well, dear, you have had a great fright; but all will soon be right again. Now go to bed and sleep, that I may take a good report of you to Clara."

Mabel turned away to leave the room, in a sort of mechanical obedience; but Frank detained her firmly by the hand.

"I will not have you blame yourself; it was no fault of *yours*."

Mabel's dark-grey eyes looked full into his. The childish sorrow, the childish expression, seemed to have vanished at once.

"Thank you!" was all she answered. Then, turning to Mrs. Stretton, "I am not at all tired, aunt. May I not go now and sit with Catherine?"

Mrs. Stretton hesitated a moment. Frank again interposed :—

"Go to my sister, of course, Miss Arleigh, whenever you wish. You know she is never so happy as when you are with her."

CHAPTER XV.

"I MET Frank Calder this morning," said
Dr. Harland to his wife, on his return home
one afternoon, two or three weeks after his
hasty summons to Calder House. " He tells
me that his sister is so nearly well again, that
he has come up to London as usual. I was
afraid at first, from his looks, that there had
been a relapse; he must have been alarming
himself very unnecessarily."

The next day, when Edward arrived at the
counting-house, he found a hurried note from
Frank, begging to see him at his chambers as

soon as possible. A certain urgency in the
mode of expression rather alarmed him, and
he lost no time in complying with his friend's
request.

His first impression on seeing Frank was
the same as Dr. Harland's had been.

" Is your sister worse ?" was his involuntary exclamation.

" What ! Is anything the matter ? Have
you heard anything ?" and he seemed ready
to hurry off in a sort of bewildered alarm.

" *I* have heard nothing ; all is right, of
course, if *you* have not. But you sent for me
rather in haste."

" I recollect," said Frank, compressing his
lips, and resuming the peculiar look, which
had become habitual to him, of business-like
determination—of a set purpose to carry out
unflinchingly what he had made up his mind
to. He had the especial English character
which instinctively strives to meet difficulties
as trifles, and to conceal the strongest excite-

ment under the practical commonplace guise
of ordinary business.

"Just sit down a minute. Will you not
have luncheon?" He was opening the door
to give orders.

"Nothing, thank you. A splendid day, is
it not?"

"Splendid. You remember hearing that
my father died just before — I came of
age!"

"I have heard so from Harland."

"Near the end he wished to speak to me
alone." He stopped short.

"Very natural," was all Edward could
think of in reply.

"Then he told me—no wonder it killed
him—that is—you know he could not have
borne all that was to go forward on *that* day."
Another painful pause, which Edward knew
not how to break.

"He told me—that I was not—that I could
not *inherit*," said Frank, turning deadly pale,

and forcing out the words between his white lips.

Edward involuntarily averted his head, colouring painfully in spite of himself; then turning round, he would have taken his friend's hand, but Frank seemed to perceive and understand nothing.

"Now, Edward,"—laying his hand almost roughly on Edward's arm—"I *will* not have you think me a villain! I was *not!*" he burst out as fiercely as if some one had contradicted him. "I told him she should have the benefit of all; that the whole rental of the estate should be her dower. I *have* kept my word, and *will!* I hate the place, and all belonging to it; and the very sight of the money! But it was too much to expect that I should bear *that!* I should have been used to it when I was a child," he added, with a sudden softening of inexpressible distress.

"My dear fellow," said Edward, warmly, "I should as soon think myself a villain as

think you one. I don't know who could have
had courage — and then, you have taken
such care of her; such pains to make her
happy !"

" I doubt if she *has* been happy, though,"
said Frank. " I suppose no good could come
of the affair, any way. And then it has been
hard to like her properly, poor child! knowing that all the world would cry shame upon
me for wronging her, if only the truth were
known; and yet that she had so much the
advantage of me in all ways—was so infi-
nitely enviable ! But the thing won't bear
talking of. Tell me what to do; I am tired ;"
he ended, wearily leaning his head on his
hand.

" I think," said Edward, in a suppressed
voice, " that if I were to have a limb ampu-
tated, I should only entreat it might be done
at once—as soon as the necessary preparations could be made."

" That's it !" exclaimed Frank, springing

up. But you must help me; I am a cow-
ard," he added, with an attempt at a smile.
And indeed he was looking quite faint; far
paler than he would have done had an actual
operation awaited him.

"You are ill," said Edward, kindly. "Put
it out of your head a bit;—no, that I know
you can't do; but leave it to me just now,—
I'll think it over, and see what can be done.
And just take a glass of wine, old fellow. It's
a horrid thing to have to do, but the finer
fellow you to go through with it."

And squeezing his friend by the hand,
Edward left the room. He saw that Frank
needed to be alone.

And solitude did more for Frank than even
sympathy could have done. As the door
closed behind Edward, he threw himself at
full length on the great horsehair sofa, face
downwards. Two or three times his robust
frame quivered all over, like some forest-tree
shaken by a whirlwind; then came a few

smothered moans, fainter and fainter; and he was asleep.

The next morning betimes Edward was again at Frank's chambers.

" Frank !" he began abruptly, " I've been thinking it over, and one thing is clear to me :—it would kill your sister to have such a shock in her present state." Frank looked aghast. " You know it *would* be a shock to her," pursued Edward; " and if the thing were once mentioned at all, it would be sure to come to her ears."

" But how am I to bear it? I cannot tread the very ground there without feeling myself an impostor. You will wonder how I have borne it so long; but when I saw her looking like death, I knew all at once what it would be if she were taken away before I had made reparation. Besides, I had not been careful enough of her; I could not be sure; it would be my doing. You may think what you please of me, but I cannot look on her face again, while I know that I am wronging her."

Edward saw instinctively that it was no case for argument.

"Only wait till she is a little stronger," he pleaded. "Then, if you think that the best way, I could go down to Ringwood, and speak to any one you thought fit. Perhaps Dr. Hinchley, whom Mabel sometimes writes about, could tell your sister quietly just as much as she *must* know, before it is mentioned farther."

Frank looked inexpressibly relieved. He had felt the communication to his sister an insurmountable difficulty.

"After all," said Edward, as a new aspect of the affair broke upon him; "after all, will it not be as well to postpone all disclosures till she is of age? It will make no practical difference to her till then; and then she will be fitter to hear it," he added, softly.

He had, indeed, been so carried away by

Frank's own view of the case,—had identified himself so completely with his friend's feelings, that this common-sense suggestion had not till that moment occurred to him.

It was, however, quite unavailing now, whatever it might have been if proposed earlier. Frank's mind was now immovably anchored on the fixed idea of immediate restitution ; or rather, perhaps, of speedy deliverance from the mental burden which had been so long weighing down his life, and which had suddenly become too heavy for him to bear.

Edward saw in a moment that it was useless to press the point.

" Very well," he said, soothingly, " it shall be as you please ; — as soon as she is strong enough."

" But I cannot go down there till it is done," persisted Frank, somewhat doggedly.

" No, I understand ; you had much better stay here quietly till it is all settled," Edward was beginning; but his heart smote him as he saw Frank's half-despairing glance round the large, gloomy room, become hateful to him from the mental struggles with which it was associated.

" Could you come to us?" he suggested, timidly. He instinctively anticipated Frank's ill-concealed shrinking from the proposal. " No, that won't do,—we must think of something else. You can't stay here alone, that is clear."

There was a tap at the door; and a clerk entered, laden with letters, which Frank impatiently signed to him to put down on a high desk close by.

When the man had left the room, however, he mechanically turned the letters over, passing them slowly through his fingers, in the pre-occupation of his thoughts. Suddenly he started. " From Mrs. Stretton!" he exclaimed, as he caught sight of the handwriting; and he grew pale as in the torture of the previous day's confession. But he uttered an ejaculation of relief as he glanced over the contents; and almost smiled before he reached the conclusion.

" My dear Sir,"—Mrs. Stretton wrote—

" Catherine is better, nearly well; so you need not be alarmed at the sight of my hand-writing. Yet I do actually write to recall you. We are in great trouble and perplexity. The river-wall of the favourite conservatory has given way; it is feared that the workmen employed last year in the repairs must have injured the foundation, which has consequently been unable to resist the action of the water. You know how much the stream was swollen in the winter months. Old Roberts rushed in yesterday morning, breathless and aghast, to announce to us the calamity. Poor Catherine was sadly vexed, more so than I have ever seen her about anything of the sort; but this has been a hobby of hers. And this morning she begs me to write to you, and ask you, if possible, to come down and see about it. This really seems an inconsiderate whim on her part, as you are doubtless much occupied, and have already had so much trouble on account of her accident; she appears herself half-ashamed of her request; and I believe it is chiefly an excuse for persuading you to return, as she has missed you a good deal. So there is no need to inconvenience yourself, should your engagements make it difficult for you to come down.

"Yours truly,

"JANE STRETTON."

"I shall go down directly," was Frank's only comment, as Edward handed him back the letter.

Edward looked doubtful, but did not expostulate. "Remember to be careful," was all he said.

CHAPTER XVI.

In little more than a week after Frank's return to Calder House, his secret was known, or rather, was beginning to be known, in the neighbourhood. A few of the leading gentlemen having been taken into confidence, had been requested to make the tidings quietly, but distinctly, understood in their respective districts.

The news created less sensation than might have been expected. Frank was little personally known, except by the immediate dependents of the family; and to these, at least until Catherine came of age, the affair would make little practical difference. Miss Calder had grown up in the place, and for some time past it had been pretty generally understood that her wishes were law on the estate. And the rustic mistiness, which pervaded by far the greater number of brains in that remote region, was not favourable to distinct conceptions on any subject not immediately affecting the material interest of the day.

Now and then, indeed, some labourer, opening a gate for Frank's horse to pass through, bestowed on "the master" a rather inquisitive glance, as if expecting to see him in some way altered; or some broad-shouldered farmer raised his hat with unusual respect as he passed Mr. Calder in some narrow lane, on one of his frequent rounds of inspection. But he always *had* managed the estate, and of course he did so still; there was nothing to remark upon.

How the change in their relative positions
was first intimated to Catherine herself, her
brother never knew. But there was reason
for believing that Dr. Hinchley's courage had
quailed before the task which, at Frank's
request, he had undertaken ; and that he had
pusillanimously turned it over to a woman.

Want of courage had certainly never been
one of Mrs. Stretton's faults. No one would
have suspected her of shrinking from a difficult duty. But no one would have previously
believed her capable of breaking the news to
the poor girl so gently, so tenderly, that neither
health nor spirits received any lasting shock.
When Catherine first learnt it, even Frank's
jealous watchfulness could not trace ; he only
gradually became certain that she *had* learnt
it, by the lingering pressure with which she
now often held fast his hand, detaining him
for hours beside her sofa, instead of merely
following him with wistful eyes when he was
about to leave the room.

Once only was the subject alluded to between them; when Catherine, as if by some sudden, irresistible impulse, put her arms round her brother's neck, with the words:—

"Frank! dear Frank! why cannot all things go on as they were before? I should be so much happier."

But he broke away from her so vehemently, that she at once retracted her rash speech.

"Do not go, Frank! pray do not! It shall be just as you wish; I will not say anything more about it."

Frank stooped down and kissed her forehead.

"Thank you, dear, for what you wished to say; but you do not know—you cannot understand. It is *impossible;* will you remember that?"

"So Mrs. Stretton said," murmured Catherine, almost to herself.

Frank half started; but only replying— "So you see, dear, it *cannot* be," he at once and decidedly changed the subject.

And, indeed, Mrs. Stretton's own view of the matter had been so strong—she had so forcibly urged upon Catherine the impossibility of carrying out her wishes in her brother's favour—the folly, and consequently the cruelty of even proposing such a scheme to himself— that Catherine, with a heavy heart, had acquiesced; and was now not a little shocked and ashamed at the unconsidered impulse which had urged her, against her resolutions, upon the forbidden topic.

Mrs. Stretton's own manner, always more unconstrained and cordial with Frank than with most people, continued precisely what it had always been. But she was now less and less at Calder House; Catherine was by this time so nearly recovered, that Mrs. Stretton's watchful superintendence was no longer needed; and she kept Mabel with unusual strictness to her studies, which, since the accident, had been wholly suspended. So Mabel could only be spared to sit with her friend occasionally, when, from some unavoidable absence of Frank's, Catherine was in especial need of society.

And for a time it really seemed as if neither brother nor sister had leisure to miss her. Catherine was so anxious, by constant companionship, to ward off all annoyances from Frank, or, at least, to prevent his dwelling upon them; while he seemed almost unconscious of any, in the sense of relief from a heavy burden. Despite the many painful circumstances which no watchful affection could avert, he was at times almost what Catherine remembered him first in his light-hearted, boyish days.

If he did indeed remark the almost total suspension of intercourse with the Chace, he at least made no remark upon it to his sister; it might have been fancied, by any close observer, that he almost studiously avoided drawing Catherine's attention to the subject. One day, however, they were discussing the repairs needed to put the conservatory once more in order. Though the disaster there had been made the plea for his recall, its consideration had been postponed to the far deeper interests which had intervened. Now, however, the matter was becoming urgent. The foundations were in so insecure a state that, unless prompt measures were adopted, the whole building might speedily give way.

"And that would vex Mabel so sadly," observed Catherine. "She has taken such a fancy to the old place. But how long it is since Mabel has been here!" she added, with sudden recollection. "It is a great pity she is so busy now with her lessons. I do not believe, Frank, that you have seen her once since you came home last."

A momentary silence followed her remark; she looked up questioningly. But her brother spoke as if he had not been attending to what she had just said.

"Catherine, you are not at all strong yet;

do you not think it would be a good thing if I were to take you abroad for the winter?"

"My dear Frank, how pleasant!"

"Then I will go up to town to-morrow, and talk to Harland about it. If he approves, I can make all arrangements; and you and Mrs. Elliott can meet me there, as soon as you are ready to start.—I am afraid I shall not be able to come down again and fetch you," he added, in reply to Catherine's half-disappointed look; "but I will give all orders, so that you may have no trouble. You had better travel slowly, and sleep on the road. I will order beds and post-horses at the proper stages, if I find that Dr. Harland thinks the plan a good one for you at all."

CHAPTER XVII.

What a different winter was this to Mabel
from the last! Catherine's letters certainly
were an unmixed delight ;—she was so happy,
and had such wonders to relate ! But Mabel
felt as if her companion had been carried from
her into fairy-land. A golden haze surrounded
Catherine's image in her imagination ; but she
herself was still in grey, sober England ; was
still a girl in the school-room ; was alone with
her aunt and Fräulein C.

Quietly, almost gravely, she went through
her routine occupations ; worked really hard,

for the first time in her life, at her lessons; took her regular walks and regular rides;— seeming rather glad than otherwise of Fräulein C.'s companionship in the former; and submitting, with perfect acquiescence, to the attendance of the groom, who now always followed her in the latter.

Arthur, indeed, came home as usual for the Christmas holidays. But he was just verging upon the unsociable, half-sulky stage of boyhood. He had, besides, some tough examination to prepare for; and was also beginning to devote himself to painting with a sort of business-like earnestness. So he was altogether much less of a companion to Mabel than formerly; and as she went on quietly with her usual practising, drawing, writing, and reading, these Christmas holidays scarcely formed any break in her ordinary way of life.

Her health, however, continued as perfect as ever. She grew taller, and even rather prettier. Still Mrs. Stretton did not quite like the calm, self-contained manner,—the something almost like womanhood, which seemed so suddenly to have superseded childhood. She had always been more observant of her niece than it was in her nature to show; and now she watched, more anxiously than any could have guessed, for some girlish outburst, some demonstration of eager interest, such as she might formerly have discouraged as undignified and absurd. She really longed to catch from Mabel some unguarded expression of any strong desire which she might gratify her by fulfilling.

She watched and waited long; it came at last.

"Oh, aunt! Clara's baby!—If I could only see Clara's baby!"

Mrs. Stretton remained silent for a few minutes.

"Mabel," she then began, in a thoughtful, calculating tone, "if you could spend only a

few hours with your friends, would it content
you?"

"Oh, aunt! would you really be so kind?"

"I have been thinking," pursued Mrs.
Stretton, "that we must travel a little, Mabel,
like other people." Mabel absolutely sprang
from her chair. "Only in England," continued Mrs. Stretton, with a quiet smile at
her delight; "I am too old,—or too old-
fashioned, at least,—to have anything to do
with strange lands. But the point is this:
on our way we must pass through London,
and I must remain there a day on some particular business. If *you* like to spend the day
with Mrs. Harland, you shall do so." Mabel
sprang up and kissed her aunt, towards whom
she was rarely impelled into any special de-
monstrations of affection. "We must start in
a week or two," said Mrs. Stretton, "that we
may have the summer before us. When I
can fix the time, you may write and let Mrs.
Harland know. I think we must give Fräu-

lein C. a holiday of a few months," she
added. "No doubt, she will be glad enough,
having been tormented with you so long."

The week or two were extended to upwards
of a month; it was no slight matter for Mrs.
Stretton to leave Ringwood. Since her residence abroad, in the first days of her marriage — that is, since the Chace had become
her own—she had never quitted it except for
a few days, and those at very distant intervals; and it seemed difficult to herself and to
her numerous dependents to imagine how
things could go on there without her, for, it
might be, two or three months. Day by
day passed, and found her still fully occupied,
giving minute instructions to her steward, examining personally every detail of management, looking over old account books and
papers; not that anything really required
what is commonly understood by "putting
in order;" such an expression would have
sounded absurd to any one acquainted with

Mrs. Stretton's habits. But travelling was
not in those times such an every-day matter
as it is now; even the least timid or super-
stitious felt, when on the eve of a journey, a
certain awe, which led them, if not actually to
make or alter their wills, at least to set their
house in order, literally as well as figuratively,
from a vague sensation of doubt as to their
ever returning thither in safety.

Some such unacknowledged feelings may
have induced Mrs. Stretton, over and above
the needful business arrangements, to look
over and re-sort the accumulations of old
papers stowed away in the homely walnut
bureau, once her father's, now her own private repository for writings connected with
the past, and not liable to be wanted in the
current affairs of the day. Even here, however, no sentimental memorials found a place.
The faded love-letters of her father and mother, the school scrawls of her boy, the few
epistolary records of her own married life, all

reposed in the small sandal-wood cabinet which stood beside her bed. She *knew* that they were there, and that sufficed ; she *never* looked at them. Even in her examination of the other more matter-of-fact hoards, she seemed instinctively to seek an excuse for herself; there was always some good reason, even to her own mind, why some particular paper was at that moment important, and must be sought for among those rarely-touched tokens of the past.

" Mabel," said Mrs. Stretton one morning, turning back, just as she was on the point of leaving the breakfast-table, " you were out the other day, and I did not know where to send for you, or I could have shown you something that might have interested you."

Mabel looked up, with some curiosity, but with a much more quiet and subdued expression than had been her wont, in her days of childish eagerness.

" Do you remember how full you were once

of the story about the twin-brothers and the picture?" inquired Mrs. Stretton, with an evident desire to arouse her attention.

"Oh yes! I remember, of course. Have you found out anything about it, aunt?"

"The other day, I was looking back for something respecting a lease, among some old letters of my father's, and when I untied a bundle of them, just put carelessly aside, out fell something that looked quite different; and when I examined it more narrowly, it proved to be the very letter from the elder brother, which we have never been able to find. (My dear father never was methodical in such things.) I was sorry you were not in the way, as you might have liked to see it; but I could not wait, so I locked it up at once in the fire-proof safe."

"I wish I had seen it," said Mabel. "But did it tell the name of the place where the farm—where the picture was?"

"Yes—I suppose so; it was dated 'Merston.' I never heard of such a place, but perhaps we may find out."

"Then we may really find the picture!" exclaimed Mabel, her eyes lighting up. "Oh, I do wish I had not been out just then!"

"There was nothing particular in the letter, only what you have heard before," said Mrs. Stretton, "except, indeed, one curious thing. The elder brother relinquishes his claim in favour only of his twin-brother, and children, if he had any (which you know he had not). So it is not an absolute surrender, as was taken for granted."

Mabel looked puzzled.

" I mean," explained Mrs. Stretton, " that had this elder brother left any descendants, *they* would have been the rightful heirs to the estate, instead of my grandfather and ourselves."

"But, aunt, perhaps he did leave some children! I thought you told me that nobody knew whether he did or not?"

"Nobody thought of enquiring at the time; but it is not likely, or they would some of them have made their way back to the old place."

"Poor things! perhaps they were left forlorn and destitute!"—and Mabel's eyes filled with tears.

"My dear, they must have known perfectly well to what family they belonged, and would have applied for help if they had wanted it."

Mabel still looked uneasy.

Her aunt took her hand affectionately.

"My dear Mabel, set your good little heart at rest; to relieve your anxiety, I will tell you what I have never mentioned to any one before. My dear, kind-hearted father was uneasy, as you may be, at the possibility of children having been left destitute; so he spared no pains in inquiring, through proper agents, as to whether there were, or had been, any descendants. You know the name would be the same; so the thing could easily be traced ; and had any descendants existed, they were not likely to have neglected claiming kinship with the Strettons of Ringwood."

Mabel remained silent and pondering.

" I see what you are thinking of, Mab. Come, now I will really tell you *all*—more than I ever thought to tell anyone. The agent whom my father employed did make inquiries, amongst others, of your friend Mrs. Harland's grandfather."

Mabel started.

" He was then a rich, eccentric old gentleman, living in a splendid house, adjoining his place of business, in the darkest, most crowded part of the city. He was well known, and used to boast how his father and himself had been the architects of their own fortune. The name, of course, made him one to be applied to on the subject. But he quietly returned the letters addressed to him, refused any personal interview, and merely wrote to beg that he might be troubled with no impertinent investigation into his descent; that there was no family, however high they might hold themselves, whom he had any wish or pretension to call cousins. Mabel, I have told you this for your satisfaction. I did not know it myself, till lately I came upon a whole mass of correspondence relating to the affair. But I must rely upon your honour not to mention it in any way to your friends."

"Of course, aunt, I will not mention it if you desire me not. I am not quite so self-willed as I was once, I hope,"—and she laughed involuntarily, as a former scene with her aunt, upon the subject of the picture, flashed upon her remembrance. "But I may tell them the name of the place, may I not? They really *ought* to know about *that*. And then"—she smiled somewhat roguishly as she concluded—"*then* they might help us to find the picture."

Mrs. Stretton laughed in her turn.

" You are a cunning little diplomatist, Mab, and generally manage to get your own way. You may tell them the name of the place, if nothing else will satisfy you; but mind, the other affair concerns ourselves only, and I *will* not have it talked about. But we have no more time to discuss such matters now; in a few days, you know, we are to leave home."

The weeks had passed lingeringly as they went; yet Mabel was almost surprised when the time of preparation was really expired. The interval had been to her external senses little more than a blank. Her mental vision had seen only Clara.

CHAPTER XVIII.

"Aunt, I have been very wicked!"

Mrs. Stretton did not often start; but there was some excuse for her doing so at Mabel's sudden utterance of these portentous words.

"My dear Mabel! how can you exclaim in that absurd way? What can you possibly mean?"

"I mean, aunt, that I had forgotten all about poor grandmamma and grandpapa!"

A very remarkable change passed suddenly over Mrs. Stretton's countenance. She looked positively conscience-stricken.

" I ought to go and see them, you know," pursued Mabel, "before I go to see any one else; before—instead of—going to Clara,—if you can only stay one day in London?"

" Well, I won't be quite so hard as that upon you, Mab! I will stretch a point, and stop a second night at the hotel. The first day you shall go and see your grandpapa and grandmamma, of course; you are quite right."

Mrs. Stretton made a long pause, as if scarcely able to make up her mind as to what was to follow.

" Do you wish that I should go too?"

" Oh no, thank you, dear aunt! I mean, you are very, very kind; only—"

" I understand,"—and she stroked Mabel's hair almost caressingly. " But I should have been sorry not to show all the respect in my power to your father's family. Don't explain, dear,"—interrupting Mabel's confused apologies—" I know all that you mean. It would only revive painful recollections, instead of giving them pleasure." She kissed Mabel, and left the room.

It cannot be denied that Mabel's face, after this conversation, resumed much of that graver expression which it had begun to wear before the notion of the journey had been first suggested; that she went through the bustle of departure, less with a child's exhilaration at the prospect of change, than with a woman's aspect of determined purpose. She, perhaps, looked back more lingeringly than she might otherwise have done at the lodge-gates, remembering, with sudden distinctness, all that had passed since she first entered them that dreary autumn evening. Throughout the journey, which she now retraced under such altered circumstances—so altered, too, in herself and her feelings—she remained unusually thoughtful. It needed the bewildering excitement of re-entering London, so long unvisited, and the overpowering sleep of utter weariness at a London hotel, to restore her to a natural consciousness of outward realities.

Not a word farther had passed between Mrs. Stretton and her niece on the subject of Mabel's proposed visit ; but directly after breakfast the carriage was ordered, to take Miss Arleigh to Bellevue Terrace.

It was a simple act ; yet, perhaps, it cost Mrs. Stretton more than many deeds which are dignified with the epithet of " heroic." The same *name* even ! But she did it quietly, as she did everything, and made no sign.

And Mabel? Perhaps she was by this time awakening to some slight consciousness on such points ; perhaps her heart sank a little when the carriage left the pleasant streets, squares, and parks for the dusty roads, the blocks of half-finished houses, the mean-looking, straggling " rows," which reminded her of Bellevue Terrace.

It was only a passing cloud. The nearer she found herself to the home of her earliest-known relatives, the warmer grew her heart at the prospect of the meeting; at the thought of the real affection and self-sacrificing kindness bestowed in time of need upon herself and her little brother. She began really to long for the warm greeting, the fond embrace, which, she could not doubt, awaited her.

She was doomed to something like disappointment. In her reception, it could not be denied, a shade of coldness was perceptible. She was hardly now, to the old couple, their own little Mab; they could not quite forget her new position, so different from the sphere in which their own lives had been passed; so disproportionately imposing in their eyes, seen through the misty medium of their imperfect worldly knowledge. They could scarcely think of her now except as "Miss Arleigh" of Ringwood.

A little of the same feeling had imperceptibly marred their pleasure in Arthur's first visit; but he had been so much more their

own child, and was still so completely a little
boy, that it passed off, before he could be
conscious of any change, except such greater
indulgence as was natural after a long separation. But Mabel's warm nature and quick
instincts at once perceived and recoiled from
the altered manner.

"Dear grandmamma, do pray leave off
being *polite* to me! I shall think you have
really forgotten me, and actually mistake me
for some one else! Grandpapa! won't you
scold me a little *wee* bit, just to make me feel
at home? Not too much, you know;—I
never liked that, did I?"

The old couple only half understood her
words; but her looks, tones, and *ways*, so
entirely her old self, did more than any words
could have done. They became more easy
with her, more cordial; and she soon perceived that the relief from cares and respon-
sibilities, too heavy for their years, had really
in some measure counterbalanced the wearing

effect of time. There was more habitual
cheerfulness, more hopeful enjoyment of life.
They entered with real pleasure and interest
into the long accounts which she gave them
of her own and Arthur's doings; of the daily
life at the Chace. The pressure of pecuniary
anxiety, of perpetual, disheartening struggle,
had been removed by Mrs. Stretton's entire
adoption of the children. They were now in
easy circumstances, according to their habits
of life; the souring, fretting influence of po-
verty no longer embittered their tempers, or
contracted their hearts. They could scarcely
harbour unfriendly feelings towards one who
so cherished their poor Robert's children, and
to whose timely intervention they themselves
indirectly owed the repose and comfort of
their latter years.

So Mabel soon felt that all was right,
and really enjoyed the little dinner, of
grandmamma's own best cooking; and at
which grandpapa insisted upon helping her,

Mabel, to whatever he thought particularly nice.

" I am so glad you like it, my dear," observed the old lady, in evident relief. " I saw to it all myself to-day ; though generally, now, I can pretty well trust Nancy, and have no need to worry about things, only just in the way of amusement. You would hardly have known Nancy, would you, Mabel?—Grown quite a woman, is she not? And I have really made something of her at last, in the way of a servant. I am sure no one need despair, after that ; for a more careless—but you remember, don't you, my dear, what a hand I used to have with her?"

And by-and-bye came tea, set out in great state in the best parlour—unprecedented honour !—with the real old china tea-service, and silver tea-pot, and curious little silver tea-caddies, all which had formed part of the old couple's wedding outfit; and hot, buttered toast, and a cake of grandmamma's making.

R 2

And Mabel began to feel so snug and home-like, and her descriptions of her rides and her lessons, of her governess and of Catherine, were so intensely interesting to her hearers, that the whole trio were thoroughly surprised, and not a little sorry, when the carriage came to the gate, and it was found (notwithstanding some attempts on grandpapa's part to throw doubts on the accuracy of all clocks and watches) that the hour for Mabel's leaving was really arrived. Lingeringly and regretfully she kissed and was kissed ; turning back over and over again, to say how happy she had been, and how she hoped to come again soon.

Oh, my dear! it is all very well to talk of what you will do ; but we shall have some fine young gentleman carrying you off next, and then there is no knowing when we may catch you again," said Mr. Arleigh, with old-fashioned facetiousness. He was quite enlivened into jocularity by the unwontedly cheery day which he had enjoyed.

The hot blood rushed vehemently over Mabel's face and neck. Mr. Arleigh was quite frightened at the effect which his words had produced. " I beg your pardon, my dear, I am sure ; I did not mean to annoy you. It would be nothing but right and proper if it were so, and what we should all wish."

" Oh, no, I am not angry, dear grandpapa ; but I must not stay ; I promised my aunt to be quite ready. Good-bye ; good-bye, dear grandmamma. I *must* go."

And Mabel, breaking from her grandmother's detaining embrace, hurried down the little stone pathway into the carriage. The old people strained their eyes, till her waving hand was no longer visible.

CHAPTER XIX.

"I SHALL call myself for you at Dr. Harland's this afternoon," were Mrs. Stretton's parting words the next morning, as Mabel was preparing to start on her second visit.

"Oh, aunt! will you really?" But the carriage had already driven off; and in half an hour's time the vision of the preceding weeks was realized. Dear Clara! so exactly her own old self, only softer and prettier, with the white lace cap and pink ribbons over her bright black hair. And the baby! Mabel's eyes could not be satisfied with looking ;

while Clara, between her outpourings of personal happiness, was tracing with amusement the innumerable little indescribable changes which the interval of their separation had wrought in Mabel, leaving her, notwithstanding, so entirely the very same.

Dr. Harland was out, but was expected home before long.

"And papa will come round here to see you, Mab; but is it not vexatious about Edward?"

" Why, what is the matter with Edward?"

" Nothing the matter; but I thought I had told you? Oh, you cannot have received my letter; you started a day sooner than I expected. He is from home, and there was no time to let him know, or I dare say he would have come back, for the sake of seeing you."

"Oh, Clara! I am so disappointed! I did so want to see Edward; and now—there is

no knowing how long it may be. Where is
he gone?"

"Only on some provoking business of my
uncle's (*he* always manages to vex one, I think,
somehow or other). *Now* he has set his mind
on some wild patch of ground, far down in
the country, which is to make a *millionaire*
of him, I believe, if he can only get possession
of it. And the provoking thing is, that it is
my fault; we had him here to meet Wrotham, and ever since he has talked of nothing
but mining or quarrying, I really don't know
which, for I never properly listened. But
there is some difficulty about the purchase,—
the title not clear, I fancy; and he has beguiled Edward down, I can't think how, or of
what use he will be. I hope he will not
entice Edward into any of his speculations."

"Oh, Edward is not so foolish. But you
must tell him I did wish to see him so very
much. And where are the two little girls,
Clara? I want to know them."

"They are only getting ready for a walk; I am obliged to send Barlow with them, now I can't take them out myself. The poor little things don't half like it. But they will come in for me to see them before they go."

The door opened, and Janet bounded in, looking very pretty, and rather conscious, in her little pelisse and bonnet. She sprang up to Clara, and hung about her, half-hiding her face, with make-believe shyness of Mabel, at whom she cast sidelong glances every now and then between her curls.

"And where is Annie?"

"Annie is crying; she is cross."

Clara rose hastily, but her changing colour showed that the effort was too much for her.

"Let me go and bring her down," said Mabel. "Just tell me where to find her."

"She is in our bedroom, putting on her things," said Janet, "but she is cross. I daresay she will not come down."

"Janet, I am ashamed of you!" Clara looked very much annoyed.

"Will you really, dear Mab, go upstairs for me? Janet does not mean to be unkind; but she should not speak so of her sister."

The little head was pressing against her knee, and Clara, even while reproving, was involuntarily passing her hands over the long curls, which sprang back elastic from the pressure with which she straightened them for a moment.

Mabel looked on for a minute, amused and absent. Clara had done the very same thing to *her* so many times. Then, recollecting poor little Annie, she turned to seek her.

"Thank you, dear Mab. It is the first door on the right hand, at the top of the first flight. I think," she added in an under-tone, "the poor child feels forlorn now I have baby, so don't be cross with her."

Mabel smiled and nodded, and ran up stairs.

The child was standing before the glass, trying steadily to fasten her little tippet, in which she seemed to find some difficulty. And no wonder; for when, at the opening of the door, she turned slowly round, Mabel saw that the heavy grey eyes were surcharged with tears, which were making their way slowly through the thick lashes, over the colourless cheek.

They appeared to dry up at the sight of the intruder, whom the child continued to look at fixedly, with a grave, half-frightened expression.

Mabel also stood quite still. "You know," she said quietly, "she *must* love her own little baby now, better than anything else."

The child started.

"Do you know? Would you be sorry too?"

"Yes," said Mabel, slowly, as if taking time to consider, "yes; very, I think."

"You will not say anything to mamma?"

"No, of course not."

"I will put on my bonnet," said Annie, resolutely.

"Come down with me," said Mabel. "Stay, I will help you."

And she good-naturedly fastened the tippet, tied the bonnet-strings, and smoothed the disorderly hair. The servant who generally attended on the little girls, had left the room in a pet, after vainly trying to overcome "Miss Annie's sulkiness."

The child was now quickly equipped, and followed Mabel resolutely into the drawing-room. Clara was sitting on her low chair, with baby on her lap; Janet, standing by her, was holding up one pretty trifle after another, to make the little thing crow and spring toward it.

Annie went straight up to the group.

"My dear little baby brother, you shall have all my pretty things, all my picture-books; I will put all by for *you*."

Janet eagerly chimed in :—

" Yes, baby, and papa has promised me a new feather in my hat, so you shall have the old one."

While Clara and Mabel were still laughing at this outburst of generosity, Barlow came in for the " young ladies," and they were at length fairly started on their walk.

Dr. Harland came home before the little party returned. He welcomed Mabel cordially, enquired good-humouredly the latest news of Catherine, and then asked for " the children." Baby, a vigorous, strong-lunged boy, had been sent upstairs for a time, but was now recalled, to enjoy his usual plunging and crowing in his father's arms.

" And where are Janet and Annie?"

Clara explained, adding some hint of her anxiety about Annie.

"Foolish little woman !" said her father, laughing, " she will soon learn better. But what will you say to Clara herself, Miss Ar-

leigh? I warrant you have been accustomed
to think her a very sensible person. Now, a
few days after this boy's birth" (and baby received an extra toss), " I found her crying as if
her heart would break; because, she said, she
was sure she could not help loving her own
baby best! As if that were any business of
hers! I told her to leave me to manage my
own household, and that there was no fear
of my allowing her to neglect any of my
children; so she might make her mind easy,
till I called her to account." And Dr. Harland laid his hand caressingly for one moment on his wife's head.

Clara laughed, and held out her arms for
the baby; but the little fellow ungraciously
demurred, clinging tight to his more enliven-
ing nurse.

"You see how it is!" shaking her head,
with a side-glance of mock appeal to Mabel.
Then turning to a tastefully-decorated basket
which stood at her elbow, heaped with small

elegancies in the form of infantile appurtenances, she drew thence a daintily-embroidered
handkerchief, shook it out, and held it up
before Mabel's gaze.

"You see I do all honour to your wedding-
gift, Miss Mab!—at least, I hope you fully
appreciate the honour of its being devoted
to the service of this young gentleman? I
assure you, that all in the house, papa at the
head, seem to consider themselves born only
to be his submissive slaves! But, seriously,
I keep this handkerchief, dear Mab, to throw
over my boy when he is asleep, or when I
send him out for his airing—(which I must
do presently, as soon as papa can spare him).
You know, dear, I *could* not show my value
for it better—even as *your* gift. How pretty
it is!" she went on, playing with it as she
spoke, while Mabel, colouring and confused,
began some sort of apology for its defects.
"Why, I was quite astonished to find that
you could work so nicely! for it was a long

while ago, remember; you were quite a little girl
then. And how good of you to remember my
fancy for the Stretton Arrow! I do not mean
to give up my claim to it, I assure you,
though I *am* a married woman—a *femme
couverte*, you know, as they are rude enough
to call us."

"Fräulein C. said," began Mabel, timidly,
"that I should not—that it was not right—
that perhaps—"

She looked hesitatingly towards Dr. Harland.

"That of course *I* had some grand here-
ditary device of my own, which my dutiful
little wife was bound to adopt?" said Dr.
Harland, laughing. "My dear Miss Arleigh,
make your mind quite easy. Clara may enjoy
her aristocratic privileges without trenching on
my rights. I am from the *people*, my dear
young lady! Don't you wonder that I ever
coaxed this fastidious little hand into mine?"
—and his large grasp playfully closed for one

moment on the taper fingers, with their almond-shaped nails, of which Clara was rather more proud than quite befitted "a very sensible person."

"Now, poor Mary," he pursued, more seriously, addressing himself to Clara, "poor Mary was a country lassie, with farmer's blood in her veins, only one generation removed. By-the-bye, I have often wondered how she came to 'call cousins' with that high and mighty old Mrs. Calder,—your friend's grandmamma, you know," turning to Mabel. "It was on the mother's side, I fancy, that they were related ; if it was really more than a figure of speech between them. Their people belonged to the same side of the country, I believe ; and country people strain cousinship to the utmost."

"There is papa!" exclaimed Clara, as the well-known knock resounded up the stair.

Like a shot, Mabel was down in the hall. She sprang up, with her arms around Mr. Stretton's neck, as she had been used to do when a little child.

CHAPTER XX.

Luncheon soon followed—the children's dinner; at which they, by established charter, pretty much monopolized "grandpapa." But when the party rose to return to the drawing-room, their father summarily dismissed them.

"Off, you little rebels, to your own playroom! and let us see no more of you till you are sent for." Then, excusing himself on the plea of an engagement, he left Mabel and her old friends to the full enjoyment of each other's society, inquiring particularly, however, from Mabel, at what hour Mrs. Stretton proposed calling, that he might be at home to receive her.

And then ensued a long, confidential gossip — confidential, though there were no secrets to discuss; for the innumerable minute details, so delightful to hear and to relate, *must* have been suppressed, however involuntarily, in the presence of any one less intimately interested. Their triviality would then have struck the speaker, and rendered their communication impossible. Mabel nestled by Mr. Stretton's side, as in early childhood; Clara, not yet very strong, reclined on a sofa, her little work-table drawn close to her, with its pretty appurtenances in ivory and silver, her fingers busy with a fairy-like web of lace and embroidery, representing a baby's cap;— (babies wore caps in those days). The warm-tinted Venetian blinds were down, but not closed; the trees and turf of the square, still in their Spring freshness, lay in that peculiar

golden haze, into which a London atmosphere
is transmuted, in *very* fine weather, by that
great alchemist—the afternoon sun ;—and the
slanting rays stole into the room, between
bowery creepers and bright-coloured blossoms,
bringing in the fresh odours of mignonette,
and lighting up the damask curtains, the
choice pictures, and glancing statuettes.
Within, cool and shadowy, was the smaller
drawing-room, where Mabel had found Clara
established, with her baby, in the morning;
and still beyond, closing the vista, gleamed a
fair white marble statue. Mabel had dis-
cerned it, even in the first moments of eager
greeting; and as soon as she had thoughts for
anything beyond the joy of the hour, she had
darted off, even from Clara's side, to explore
the little apartment—no vulgar *boudoir*, but a
very Tribune—enshrining the gem of Dr.
Harland's collection — his beautiful wood-
nymph,—sleeping the delicious sleep of noontide, with limbs half-buried in thick herbage,

and smiling up-turned face, and hair, flung
back for heat, half-covering the arm on which
her head was pillowed. Neither the conception nor the execution could be called clas-
sical ; the thing was only inexpressibly lovely,
and was the pride of Dr. Harland's heart—
second only to his bright-eyed wife.

More than once this afternoon did Mabel
start from her seat for another inspection of
the beautiful statue. More than once, also, as
it grew later, did she peep shyly between the
spars of the Venetian blinds, as her eye caught
a glimpse of some equipage which she instinctively felt to be distinguished, though the
horses were all that she could properly appreciate. But, after each little escapade, she
nestled back to Mr. Stretton's side ; and the
conversation uninterruptedly flowed on. And
what a charming conversation it was at the
time ! how tantalizing and unsatisfactory in
the retrospect ! All subjects of real importance, of deep interest, seemed unaccountably

to have been forgotten, or passed lightly over; while those innumerable little *nothings* which had never been thought worth writing about, now overflowed and carried all before them; as a little brawling stream, when swollen by suddenly-melting snows, bears away masses of rock or uprooted trees in its course.

"Mabel," said Clara, when a little pause at length occurred, "would you not like to see the house? *my* house?" Clara did not yet receive general visitors; so they were secure from "morning calls."

"Oh, dear Clara, I should so like it; but you are not strong enough to go over it with me; that is why I did not ask."

"You had better not tire yourself, my dear," said her father, anxiously.

"Oh, it will not tire me! I am quite as strong as ever, now I have my little Mab again."

"Not such a little Mab now, though," she went on, as she ushered Mabel into her pret-

tily-draperied dressing-room. " *I* should
know you anywhere, of course ; but you are
what slight acquaintance would call, *grown
out of knowledge.*"

"Just what Barlow said to me, when I
went with her to take off my bonnet," said
Mabel, laughing.

"Well, you are prettier, dear, as well as
taller ; and more like the old portrait than I
ever thought you would be."

Mabel coloured, and made a hurried effort
to change the subject. She was just beginning
to be *conscious,* and therefore bashful, on the
subject of personal appearance ; and she had
a painful feeling about the portrait, and shrank
from any mention of it on Clara's part.

"This is the little girls' bed-room, is it
not ?" moving, as she spoke, towards a half-
open door. "I have seen this already, when I
came up to fetch Annie."

"Yes ; and here is our bed-room beyond. I
was obliged to part with their nurse ; they

were growing too old for her; so I keep them under my especial care. I must begin lessons with them again now; they have had an idle time of it since baby's birth. Here is their play-room," she continued, leading the way across a broad landing into a large, cheerful room, with wide windows, which seemed to command a view in all directions; for it was a corner-house, and Clara had insisted on appropriating its liveliest apartment to the girls.

Barlow, who had been sitting at work there, rose as Clara and Mabel entered, and left Janet and Annie to do the honours of their own domain.

"Well, Mabel," said Clara, after all its wonders had been duly exhibited and admired, "you have not half seen the house yet; and I *must* take you upstairs to see baby in his cot."

Nurse met them at the door, with warning, uplifted finger; noiselessly they stole in, and stood long in silence, fascinated by the sight of that rosy slumber, the loveliest thing in nature, lovelier far than aught in art. It was a sultry afternoon; the child's restless movements had partially displaced the coverings' and every few minutes there was some little change of posture, each attitude perfect in its fleeting grace. After a time, Mabel and Clara began to exchange remarks, in a subdued voice; baby did not seem disturbed, and they were soon in the full flow of pleasant, whispering, feminine chat, which lasted till a carriage drove up rapidly, and a knock was heard at the door.

They looked at each other, in a sort of mutual understanding; and then, as by tacit consent, both glided noiselessly downstairs, to be in the drawing-room to receive Mrs. Stretton.

Mabel, in her secret soul, had somewhat dreaded this interview; but it passed off to admiration. It was, indeed, too much a matter of form, for any of the party to give due scope to the kindly feelings which, below the surface, each really entertained for the other. But Mrs. Stretton's stately courtesy fascinated Clara ; it was exactly what she admired, and her own involuntary deference gave a peculiar gracefulness to her naturally somewhat proud bearing. Dr. Harland was frank and cordial as usual ; he had never been able in any degree to enter into the peculiar feelings which had induced a certain awkwardness between his wife and Mrs. Stretton ; and the entire absence of consciousness on his part did much to remove constraint on theirs.

But it was with Mr. Stretton that the visitor seemed to feel herself at once and entirely *en rapport.* Whether from some mystic sympathies of affinity, even if too remote to be called relationship ; whether from the genial sunshine of Mr. Stretton's own manner, in which was no self-assertion, simply because kindness and courtesy, given and received, were to him as much matters of course as the air he breathed; whether from the strong tie existing between them, in their common interest in the orphan-children; perhaps from all these causes combined, they were quickly on the footing of old and familiar friends. They were of the same generation, too, and had in common so many reminiscences, preferences, *prejudices*, the irreverent might add, which the younger race around them could neither share nor understand.

Coffee was brought in, and the conversation became general and animated.

It was with marked reluctance that Mrs. Stretton at length rose to take leave; and when, courteously but pointedly, she expressed her hope for a renewal of intercourse at Ringwood, even Clara could not summon an ungracious reply.

"We shall be from home for two or three months," added Mrs. Stretton; "when we are again at the Chace, Mabel shall write, and try her power of persuasion."

"And oh, aunt!" said Mabel, "may I go and say good-bye to Annie?"

"May I not see your little daughters, Mrs. Harland?"

The children were rung for. Their entrance caused a little further sociable lingering; and when Mabel had at last courageously turned away from Clara, Annie's eyes followed her so wistfully, that she paused to give her another parting kiss; and Mrs. Stretton, who was just leaving the room, turned to say good-naturedly—

"You must ask mamma to bring you to visit Mabel at Ringwood."

CHAPTER XXI.

EDWARD had been induced to leave town by the following brief note from his uncle :—

" MY DEAR EDWARD,

" Have I not heard you speak of some interest your family have in tracing out certain points of pedigree? If I am correct in my remembrance, you had better join me here at once. Perhaps I may be able to throw some light on the subject."

A few explanations as to route, conveyances, &c., concluded the note. Such friendly hints were necessary in those old coach days, when there was no "Bradshaw" to make travelling easy to the meanest capacity.

Edward, decidedly curious, and just then tolerably at leisure, was very well disposed to set off at once. He travelled deliberately, however, seeing all of interest that lay on the route. Excursion trains were not yet, and an opportunity, once missed, might never recur.

When he joined his uncle in the little inn at Stainton, he found on the table Clara's note, announcing Mabel's promised visit.

With a hastily muttered summary of its purport, he walked to the window, looking considerably chafed and annoyed.

"A very lucky chance, Edward," said Mr. Hurburne. "It would have been awkward to meet just now; much better deferred, until you are in a different position."

"What *do* you mean?" said Edward, his

colour still heightened with annoyance, and looking full into Mr. Hurburne's face.

"Why," said the latter, with some awkwardness of manner, " you would be on quite a different footing with all that family — if you could present yourself as a relation."

Edward winced, but checked some impatient rejoinder which seemed rising to his lips.

"My dear Edward," pursued his uncle, with unusual frankness and cordiality of manner, "in asking you to join me here, I had in view the advantage of both. I am inclined to hope that your own views in life may be materially furthered, while you render me a service of some importance."

"Pray come to the point, sir," interrupted Edward, impatiently.

" Well, you know, I want to purchase that bit of ground I was speaking to you about. I have had Wrotham down here, and he is quite confirmed in his former opinion. I gave him a charge, of course, to keep the thing snug; in fact, it is a bit of waste, unprofitable land, which ought to be had for a song. Perfectly useless to any one, without the capital requisite for working it."

" Well," said Edward, as Mr. Hurburne paused.

" Well, the first thing, while we were surveying, comes a whole swarm upon us from a parcel of cottages scattered round about. It was common ground, they said, and not even the lord of the manor dared enclose it. They had fed their pigs and their donkeys there all their time, and their fathers before them. ' Who was this lord of the manor?'— 'Why, Squire Hawkins, of course.'—' Where did he live?' Not a straight-forward answer could I get,—all sorts of shifts,—so at last I pretended to stroll away; and then got a rough boy, who knew nothing of the matter, to show me the house."

" And how did you succeed with Squire

Hawkins?" said Edward, in a tone of rather forced interest.

"A strange old fellow; you must see him; but the point is, that he holds that land, in some absurd way, in trust for some obsolete family of Strettons;—must not sell it away, or part with it at all, except to one of them. But it will be convenient, you know, Edward, if you can make your claim good. May be a good thing for you too; you may lay a finger on Ringwood—who knows? and make that pretty little girl glad to come into the bargain."

Edward suddenly stood up at his full height.

"Once for all, uncle; one more speech of this kind, and I am off to town again to-night."

Mr. Hurburne looked for one moment as if some sarcastic rejoinder were hovering about his lips; but after a hasty glance at Edward's face, his whole manner altered.

"My meaning, Edward, was merely to prove to you that I consider your interest no less than my own, in the trouble I take in this affair. In fact, it may be incalculably more important to you than to me. Shall I go on?"

"Pray do," said Edward, resignedly.

"Well, it seems that the very house the good gentleman lives in belongs to this same property; left in trust with his father, or grandfather, or some one, for some Stretton or other, or his representatives, should such ever be forthcoming. The property itself is not worth speaking of, a mere shred, which might be torn off Hawkins' estate, and never missed. But he has settled himself down with all snug about him, and kicks at the idea of being turned out; though he has a good house of his own, higher up the hill. (*This* is a queer old place, literally in a hole.) And it seems he has been worried, years ago, by some claimant, whose claims came to nothing; but the old gentleman's mind got harassed and unsettled at the very notion, and now he won't give any information, or enter on the subject. He cut me short in the roughest manner; but if you can bring *positive* proofs, he *must* give up; in fact, he committed himself so far as to let out that in such a case no resistance would be offered."

"Poor old man!" said Edward; "what should I harass him for, even if I had a shadow of claim?"

"There it is! you need not harass him, of course; only authorize him to make over that bit of waste ground. We would have it fairly valued; and, what is more, I should not mind pledging myself to a certain per-centage on what profits I might make; or you might even be partner with me in the speculation, if you preferred, and were prepared to share the risk."

Edward fairly laughed.

"My dear uncle, do not give yourself so much trouble! You should have the land, and welcome, on very moderate terms, if I had anything to do with it; and the poor old man might keep his house over his head! But if *he* will give no information, and *I* possess none, I don't see what light is likely to be thrown on *my* family matters—the only interest for me in the business."

"Have I not heard you say," enquired Mr. Hurburne, "that your great-grandfather was educated in the endowed school of his native place?"

"Yes; Holmfirth."

"Hum! Holmfirth;—and this is Stainton. Well, names often change. However, there *is* an endowed school here."

"Very likely."

"I made a point of ascertaining *that* before I sent for you. And yesterday I ascertained that there is to be a meeting of the trustees to-morrow, at the town-hall."

"Very well. Am I to walk into the room, and ask them after my great-grandfather?"

"You might at least ask them to refer to their books, and ascertain if any one of the name was scholar here about that time."

Edward looked a little more aroused to interest. "There can be no objection to that, certainly."

"Certainly not. Will you take anything more?" for the uncle and nephew, while conversing, had been partaking of one of those nondescript and most agreeable meals generally provided for an arriving traveller. "No? Well, then, shall we take a stroll and look about us? It is a beautiful evening, and we have an hour's daylight yet."

The thriving, unpicturesque little town looked its best in the softened evening glow; so did the bleak upland moor to which Mr. Hurburne presently led the way; expatiating with unction on its capabilities, while Edward looked around almost in bewilderment; so completely had one sudden turning of a hill, and one abrupt pitch of the rough road, left the human ant-hill out of sight or imagination. The wild scream of the sea-gull perfectly startled him; for he had travelled to Stainton by a circuitous inland route, and did not know that it was so immediately upno the coast. Indeed, the sea, having retreated considerably, had reduced the place, for all practical purposes, to an inland town; and as such the few slight allusions which had reached him had led him to consider it.

"But I do not see the sea," he observed, looking vainly round. Nothing but moorland, undulating or rugged, in all directions; the dusky glow of evening giving a mellow indistinctness to the whole.

"You cannot see it from this point; that hill is just in the way. We will go round under it to-morrow. But now, Edward, just attend to what I am saying. This is the bit of ground I was speaking of. Just look here."

And with his wonted practical clearness he went into an elaborate explanation of its capabilities; of the signs of hidden wealth beneath the surface; of the means to be employed, the expenses to be incurred, the profits to be calculated on; till Edward found himself listening with an interest at which he was himself surprised.

CHAPTER XXII.

AFTER a good night's rest, however, scarcely a trace of the conversation seemed to remain in his mind; all the interest had certainly vanished. Mr. Hurburne would have been much discomfited, could he have seen how completely his exposition had been thrown away. Edward awoke with a sense of seaside freshness, stimulating him to the unwonted enterprise of a before-breakfast walk. He wanted to go round under the hill; and very decidedly preferred doing so alone.

Before starting, he accosted a sleepy-looking

waiter, whom he found lounging near the door.

"Do you know of any place called Holm-firth near here ?"

" Beg pardon, sir.   What name ?"

" Holmfirth."

" I'll enquire, sir.—No, sir " — (after a brief absence) — " no such place hereabouts, sir."

" Has the town itself always been called Stainton ?"

" I'll enquire, sir.—Yes, sir " — (after the same process).   " None here knows of no other name.   I'm a stranger here myself, sir."

Edward gave up the point, and sallied forth. Taking a path which diverged at right angles from the one they had followed the evening before, he soon found himself on the other side of the projecting hill, which had then impeded his view.

It was a strange, wild region—miles of half-reclaimed marsh, which had once been open sea, and which still seemed, in its level blue greenness, to welter round the base of the bold rocky heights, now rising abruptly some miles inland, as formerly from the edge of the waves. From the mouth of a ravine which ran far up between these heights, burst forth a river, full, clear, and strong, quickly to lose itself in innumerable small branches, and soak beneath the surface in invisible channels. The deposit of river-mud, however, had formed along its whole course a broad belt of bright green, intensely vivid amid the surrounding greyish vegetation, and glittering with the network of tiny channels, as if bespread with dewy autumnal gossamer.

A little half-deserted village nestled close under the heights, on what had once been the angle formed by river, rock, and sea. The inhabitants had been almost entirely fishermen; and their descendants had gradually forsaken the spot, as the waves, their faithless comrades, had forsaken it.

A projecting shoulder of the hill, jutting far out into the river, formed a rough background to the desolate-looking cluster of huts which it seemed to bar off from the civilized world.

Much nearer to the present sea-marge, in a little oasis of tolerably cultivated fields, stood a small, square white house, perfectly blank and unshadowed, but evidently in such scrupulous repair as to leave no doubt of its being regularly inhabited. While Edward was wondering what sort of people could endure life in such utter isolation, or even bear the bleak winds and scorching sunshine beating by turns on the unsheltered house, a man came by, with a barrow heaped with shining wet sea-weed, which he had been collecting at low water far out upon the shore.

"Whose house is that?" Edward inquired.

"What, the Warren, sir? That be Squire Hawkins's, of course."

" Has he lived here long ?"

" Lived here, sir ? He was born in the house, and like to die there,—for he never stirs half-a-dozen miles from home,—never sleeps out of his own bed, sir, as I hear say. But you know him, sir, most like."

" No," said Edward ; " I was never here before."

" Beg pardon, sir ; so many of the quality knows each other, like."

" I do not know Mr. Hawkins," said Edward, laughing ; " but I may, perhaps, have to call upon him on business."

The man shrugged his shoulders, and gave a long, low whistle.

" What do you mean ?" said Edward ; " will there be any difficulty ?"

" Rather you than me, sir, to tackle Squire Hawkins on business. But perhaps he might be different with a gentleman."

" Do you mean—"

" I mean no harm of him, sir ;—pays his

bills and keeps his word, and employs any poor men out of work ; but a gentleman that won't be put out of his way for no one nor nothing. Good day, sir,"—-and giving his barrow a jerk, he pushed on over the rough ground.

After breakfast, Mr. Hurburne was urgent on the subject of the board-meeting; it was an opportunity which might not again occur, &c. In compliance with his wishes, and with some curiosity on his own part, Edward presented himself before the half-dozen elderly gentlemen who acted as trustees ; and inquired if the name of Hugh Stretton, as a scholar, were to be found in their books.

The old gentlemen courteously offered the books for his inspection ; but, alas ! their imperfect and dilapidated state defied research.

" Hugh Stretton ?" said one of the eldest members of the board—a hale, fresh-coloured septuagenarian, with polished bald crown, and circlet of white hair like swansdown;—"it seems, too, as if I ought to know that name. Don't you remember "—(with a sudden recollection, turning to a shrivelled old man, who, however, was ten years his junior)—"don't you remember something——Was not that very singular case, where the old woman gave evidence, something about a Stretton?"

"Ah! yes, yes!—now you remind me;—yes, certainly, to be sure! But I can't bring the particulars to mind;—and the old woman must be dead long since. Why, yes; she was the only one in the place old enough to remember the marriage——and that must be twenty years ago."

"Was it old Dame Winthorpe?" asked a lively, decided-looking man, somewhat younger than the others.

"That's the name!" exclaimed the first speaker. "Did you know her?"

"I know her now. She is hale and sound, and as capable of giving evidence as ever."

" Can we see her?" asked Edward, eagerly.

" Yet, perhaps," he added, hesitating, " it would be a risk at her age."

" My good sir, her nerves are as strong as yours, or mine either," with a look that implied, *that* is saying a good deal. " I will give you a line to her daughter ; but you will find it a pleasant ride across the country to Winthorpe Moor,—about fifteen miles, and most of it over my own property. I should be proud to mount you, if you will do me the honour ; our friends here will tell you nothing very shabby comes out of my stables. And if you will allow me, I should like to ride with you, and show you the way."

" The Winthorpes are your tenants, then ?" asked the old gentleman.

" My *neighbours!* It's well the old lady doesn't hear you, or her daughter either. Their people held Winthorpe Moor before *we* were settled at the Holms. Their land joins ours, just where the country pitches up from the flat. And good neighbours they are. I wish they skirted us all round, like a ring fence."

"They are *ladies*, then," said Edward.

"Take care they don't hear *you* say *that*," replied Mr. Allerton, laughing. "The old man used to say there never had been a gen tleman in the family yet, and he trusted in God there never would be one. And yet he was a wonderful old man. My boys used to go to him and get him to help them with their mathematics, when it was something beyond me (though I had been at college myself)— besides his knowing all about the stars, and the weather, and things of that sort, which more belong to his way of life. He left all his books to his daughter, and some of his learn- ing too, I suspect; though she keeps it snug, and takes pride in nothing but her baking and brewing (except, indeed, in the '*follow- ing*' of forty men, all kith and kin, which went out with the Winthorpe of *that* day to fight under Cromwell). As for the mother, *her* pride is in her daughter's managing the farm 'so much better than the gentry have theirs managed by their bailiffs.' They are *farmers*, not gentlefolk, sir," he added, turning to Edward, "and wouldn't change with the best of us. But when may I ride over with you, sir? Will to-morrow suit? And do you *like* a five-barred gate or two? or shall the boys be in the way to open them?"

END OF VOL. II.

Billing, Printer, 103, Hatton Garden, London, and Guildford, Surrey.

www.ingramcontent.com/pod-product-compliance
Lightning Source LLC
Chambersburg PA
CBHW020854020726
47497CB00005B/1407